"I got along fine before you showed up. I'm perfectly capable of hauling this milk can from here to there. Now move out of my way!"

"No," Creed declared, crossing his arms over his chest.

"I'm warning you, Creed Parker..."

"Don't push me, Dawn Gilbert."

"Then don't you dare holler at me. I thought diplomats were diplomatic! You probably screamed your way around the world. Now get away from my milk can! This is the United States of America, and I have my rights! I—"

"You're through, lady," he said, and in the next instant picked Dawn up and flung her over his shoulder.

"Put me down!" she demanded before switching tactics. Grabbing one of her flying braids, she danced its end across his bare, tanned back.

"Dawn! That tickles—cut it out and get out of my pants!"

Dear Reader,

Welcome to Silhouette! Our goal is to give you hours of unbeatable reading pleasure, and we hope you'll enjoy each month's six new Silhouette Desires. These sensual, provocative love stories are both believable and compelling—sometimes they're poignant, sometimes humorous, but always enjoyable.

Indulge yourself. Experience all the passion and excitement of falling in love along with our heroine as she meets the irresistible man of her dreams and together they overcome all obstacles in the path to a happy ending.

If this is your first Desire, I hope it'll be the first of many. If you're already a Silhouette Desire reader, thanks for your support! Look for some of your favorite authors in the coming months: Stephanie James, Diana Palmer, Dixie Browning, Ann Major and Doreen Owens Malek, to name just a few.

Happy reading!

Isabel Swift
Senior Editor

SDRL-7/85

ROBIN ELLIOTT
Dawn's Gift

Silhouette Desire

Published by Silhouette Books New York

America's Publisher of Contemporary Romance

SILHOUETTE BOOKS
300 East 42nd St., New York, N.Y. 10017

Copyright © 1986 by Robin Elliott

ISBN: 0-373-05303-7

First Silhouette Books printing September 1986

America's Publisher of Contemporary Romance

Printed in the U.S.A.

Books by Robin Elliott

Silhouette Desire

Call It Love #213
To Have It All #237
Picture of Love #261
Pennies in the Fountain #275
Dawn's Gift #303

ROBIN ELLIOTT

lives in Arizona with her husband and three daughters. Formerly employed in a high school library, she now devotes her time to writing romance novels. She also writes under her own name, Joan Elliott Pickart.

For Iona Lockwood and Virginia Conrad,
who shared their beautiful trees with me.

One

He was home.

Creed Parker stood at the end of the narrow dirt road, his gaze sweeping over the land, then coming to rest on the small two-story frame house nestled among the tall trees.

The old place needed a coat of paint, he mused, and the front steps were sagging, but oh, damn, it looked good. The whole farm did. Yeah, he was home.

Creed took a deep breath, filling his lungs with the early-morning air, sifting through the scents that assaulted him to see which he could still put a name to: honeysuckle, dew-soaked grass, overripe fruit on moist soil. And the sounds: squirrels chattering, birds singing, a cow or two bellowing in the distance.

He nodded in approval, then started off again, walking slowly down the road to come to the front of the house. The door would be unlocked, he knew that, but he didn't want to go in, not yet. The last streaks of dawn were giving way to the blue sky of August, with its golden sun and white clouds. The chores had begun an hour before. The house would be empty.

Creed swung his suitcase onto the wooden porch, then headed around the side of the house, his step quickening. An urgency engulfed him, a need, and he began to sprint toward the barn, his long legs covering the distance of the back lawn, then passed the chicken coops, to come at last to the weather-beaten building that was devoid of paint.

In the doorway he hesitated, allowing his eyes to adjust to the dimness. And then he saw him.

"Dad?" Creed said.

Twenty feet away a man stiffened, his back to Creed, then he slowly turned to face him.

"Creed?" he said. "My God, boy, is it really you? Creed?"

"Yeah, Dad, I ... I'm home."

"Praise the Lord. Five years. It's been five years!"

In an instant they were moving, meeting in the middle of the expanse, holding each other in a tight embrace. The son towered over the father, was bigger, stronger, tightly muscled. His hair was thick and black, with streaks of gray at the temples, while the older man's was receding some and totally gray. Eyes were matching blue, but yet, they were different. The father's eyes were warm, gentle. The son's were cold, like sentinels guarding the path to his soul.

"Creed," the man said, then stepped back, gripping his son's arms as his gaze took him in from head to toe. "You're tired."

"I was up all night."

"It's more than that."

"Yeah, Dad," he said, taking a deep breath, "it's more than that."

"Your room is just how you left it. Get some food, sleep."

"I have to unwind a little. Okay if I wander around first?"

"This is your home. You do what feels right. I gotta get these cows milked before they holler to the next county. I'll see you up at the house later."

"All right," Creed said, turning and walking to the entrance of the barn. He stopped with his back to his father. "Dad?" he said, his voice low. "Thanks...for not locking the door."

"It'll always be open for you, son. Welcome home."

Creed nodded and left the building, knowing his father was watching him go. With his hands shoved into the back pockets of his jeans, Creed went through the long, neat rows of vegetables that were ready to harvest. His broad shoulders clad in a blue chambray shirt brushed against tall stalks of corn, then he went farther to the grazing pasture, and beyond to the woods. He blanked his mind, and drank in the sights, sounds, smells of all he saw.

He was home.

Creed's wandering took him through the woods to the old swimming hole where he'd played in reckless abandon as a boy. His blue eyes flickered over the calm water, as the memories crept in on him and he stood quietly in the peaceful surroundings.

A sudden noise brought him instantly alert. He coiled, tensed, his eyes darting in all directions as he moved swiftly, silently, to the safety of the trees. He heard the breaking of twigs, the rustle of leaves,

then . . . then the lilting sound of a woman's laughter
danced across the air like tinkling wind chimes.

She emerged from the shadows of the trees to stand
in a patch of sunlight at the edge of the water, lifting
her arms to embrace the warmth brought by the passing of the dawn. Her hands floated down to untie a
blue ribbon from her hair, causing the honey-colored
cascade to tumble to her waist in silken beauty.

Creed's breath caught in his throat, as the woman
slid the knee-length terry-cloth robe from her slender
body and dropped it to the ground. She was naked,
her skin the shade of a soft, velvety peach, the gentle
slope of her hips and buttocks, the satiny length of her
long legs, declaring her to be woman, feminine, the
counterpart to Creed, the man.

His heart thundered in his chest, and a section of his
mind questioned what he was seeing, wondering if he
had imagined the vision of loveliness before him. But
then she laughed again, that delightful, free, happy
sound, and he knew she was real. She moved into the
water, then floated on her back, the fullness of her
bare breasts swelling above the surface. Her eyes
drifted closed, and an expression of serenity settled
over her delicate features, her lips holding a tiny smile.

A surge of guilt swept over Creed as he realized he
was watching what wasn't his to see. But, oh, Lord,
she was beautiful, like a nymph, a mermaid, a gift that
had come with the dawn. He felt the heat in his loins,
the stirring of his manhood, as his mind went further; saw him take her in his arms, kiss the moisture
from her skin, then lower her to the carpet of grass
and bury himself deep within the honeyed warmth of
her, making her his.

"Damn," he muttered. He had to get out of there. But who was she, this gift from the dawn? He'd leave now, grant her the privacy she assumed she had, but he had to find out who she was, where she'd come from. Was there a man waiting for her to return? Children? Surely she hadn't ventured far clad only in a robe, so she must be from a neighboring farm. Was she a wife and mother, out of his reach, beyond his touch? He had to know.

After one last lingering gaze, Creed turned and made his way back through the woods with expertise, breaking no twigs beneath his feet, causing no noise despite his large frame. He left no evidence, no trace that he had ever been there, but *he* knew. Oh, yes, he knew.

Creed looked for his father when he passed by the barn, but there was no sign of Max Parker. At the back door of the house, Creed hesitated, remembering his one-week stay of five years before. They had buried his mother, dear, loving Jane Parker, and the house had been filled with friends and neighbors bringing food, reminiscing about days gone by. Max had been consumed with grief, moving through the house in a daze, and Creed had left him like that, in the care of the neighbors. He'd had no choice, he'd had to go. Had to go back to a life, a world, his father knew nothing of, and Creed didn't want him to know.

Creed wrote to his father, just as he had done when his mother was alive. Letters of lies, of make-believe, of fantasy. He related stories of exotic cities across the globe, of beauty, splendor, excitement. He searched his imagination for descriptions of magnificent homes, parties, high fashion, anything and everything he could bring into crystal clarity on paper. But

none of it was true. None of it. He was Creed Maxwell Parker, thirty-five years old, only child of Max
and Jane. And he was a man with secrets.

He pulled open the screen door and stepped into the
yellow-toned kitchen. The gray linoleum creaked under his weight as he walked across the room, his gaze
lingering on the stove where his mother had prepared
the meals while he'd been growing up. Nothing had
been changed in the living room, and he retrieved his
suitcase from the front porch. He would take on the
memories within those walls later, when he was rested.
He was too tired now, just too damn tired.

The stairs leading to the upper rooms groaned under Creed's two hundred pounds, and the banister was
loose beneath his hand as he gripped it. He felt suddenly uncomfortable within his own body, as if he
were too big, too strong, should not be allowed to
subject the old house to who and what he was.

"Get some sleep, Parker," he said, entering a bedroom. He tugged off his shoes, tossed his shirt over a
chair and stretched out on the double bed. He sighed
deeply, shut his eyes and in the next instant was asleep.

Dawn Gilbert placed a noisy, smacking kiss on the
cheek of the gray-haired woman who was kneading
bread on the kitchen table.

"Won't do you any good," the woman said, striving to add a stern note to her voice. "I know you've
been skinny-dipping in Parkers' pond again. Max
ought to run you off with a shotgun."

"He doesn't even know I'm there," Dawn said.
"What smells so good?"

"Cherry pies. If you can bring yourself to put some
clothes on instead of just that robe, you can carry one

over to Max. Oh, and pick up his mending if there is any."

"Oh, good," Dawn said, laughing. "I get to do my Little Red Riding Hood number through the woods again with my basket of yummies. One of these days a handsome wolf is going to jump out at me."

"And what would you do with him if he did?"

"I'd think of something, Aunt Elaine," she said, wiggling her eyebrows.

"Phooey. You'd turn tail and run. You talk a fancy story, Dawn Gilbert, but you're a skittish colt when it comes to men. You've got half the males in Wisconsin tromping to the door, and you hold them all at bay."

"I'm being...selective. Better to have no man than the wrong man. That, unfortunately, I learned from experience. You see before you an older, but ever so very wiser, woman. My next husband is going to be perfection personified. A real wingdinger of a guy."

"Do tell," Elaine said, laughing softly.

"Oh, yes. In the three years since my divorce I've created the most incredible man in my mind. I'll get dressed. For all I know, he's waiting for me in the woods this very minute."

A short time later, Dawn was dressed in jeans, tennis shoes and a cotton blouse, which she tied beneath her breasts, exposing her bare stomach to any breeze she might encounter during her trek through the woods. The temperature was climbing, the humidity high, and she'd braided her hair into two pigtails to keep the heavy tresses off her neck. With a wicker basket containing the cherry pie slung over her arm, she set off in the direction of the Parker farm, a mile away.

"So much for my handsome wolf," she said when
she emerged from the woods. "Guess he's on sabbat-
ical. Yoo-hoo, Max!" she called, not really expecting
a reply.

In the kitchen, Dawn placed the pie on the table,
setting the empty basket next to it. Max Parker left any
mending he had on the chair in his bedroom, and she
dashed up the stairs. She was as comfortable in that
house as she was in Aunt Elaine and Uncle Orv's, and
Max himself seemed like part of her family.

"Blue room," Dawn said, passing the first open
door. "Green room," she said, at the second door,
then stopped dead in her tracks.

There was a man on the bed in the green room.

"Oh, good heavens," she whispered, staring into
the room.

She moved cautiously forward, halting by the edge
of the bed and peering at the sleeping figure. One
word, one thought, came to her mind: *Beautiful.* He
was absolutely beautiful. His hair was a raven glow
with streaks of gray at the temples. Temples that were
part of a tanned, rugged face with a straight nose and
square chin, accompanied by very sensuous lips. His
neck was strong, shoulders wide, arms corded in
muscles and, oh-h-h, that chest! Now *that* was a chest.
Curly black hair swirled over bronzed skin, and the
steely muscles were in perfect proportion to his arms.
Flat belly, narrow hips and, yep, nifty thighs pressed
against the faded material of his jeans. Head to toe,
the man was beautiful.

But, Dawn thought, who was he? There was a suitcase on the floor. Was he a friend or relative of Max's?
Or—oh, geez, some bum who'd found the door unlocked and wandered in for a snooze? Were bums that

beautiful? Maybe she'd better go find Max and tell him there was a beautiful bum sleeping in the green room, just in case he didn't know.

After one more appreciative appraisal of the sleeping man, Dawn turned to leave, her leg brushing against the edge of the bed. In the next instant she screamed as viselike fingers closed over her arms from behind, lifted her off her feet and flung her onto the bed. A hand gripped her throat as her body was covered by a crushing weight. With wide, terror-filled eyes, she stared up into a face that was only inches from hers.

"What?" Creed said, shaking his head slightly to clear the fogginess of sleep. "It's you! The gift...the woman...dawn. Oh, I'm sorry," he said, rolling off her and getting to his feet. "Did I hurt you?"

Dawn struggled to sit up, tugged her blouse back into place and gingerly checked her neck with her fingertips.

"Who are you?" she asked, relieved her vocal cords hadn't been smashed flat. "How do you know my name? Why are you in Max's house? Forget it," she said, scrambling off the bed. "I'm getting out of here!"

"Hold it," he said, grabbing her arm.

"Get your hand off me, Buster," she said, her voice trembling. Had that sounded tough? Brave? In control? Oh, Lord, she was scared to death!

"You're scared to death," the man said, dropping his hand. "I really do apologize. I didn't mean to frighten you. I'm Creed Parker, Max's son."

Dawn squinted at him. "You don't look like Max. Well, sort of, but you're a lot bigger. Anyway, Creed

Parker is in some foreign country being a fancy diplomat.''

"I came home," he said quietly.

Dawn looked directly up at the man, who held her
gaze unflinchingly. Her dark brown eyes locked onto
his icy blue ones, and she felt pinned in place, unable
to move. Then she realized that she was no longer
frightened, but instead, rather fascinated by this tall
man who claimed to be Creed Parker. His voice was
deep, rich, appropriate for his size, and a tiny section
of her mind wondered what it would be like hearing
him speak gentle words of love.

Slowly the web of fascination began to build as her
senses reacted to every aspect of him. There was an
awareness of his raw virility, an acute remembrance of
every steely muscle she had scrutinized, a whiff of
heady male perspiration. A strange tingling started in
the pit of Dawn's stomach and crept through her,
dancing across her breasts, causing them to ache,
showing itself finally in a warm flush on her cheeks.

And still she didn't move.

Had seconds, minutes, hours passed? She didn't
know. She saw only blue eyes that were slowly
changing, sending a message now of something different. The cold, icy stare had become one of desire.
This man wanted her!

"How did you know my name?" she asked, taking
a step backward and forcing herself to pull her gaze
from him.

"I don't know your name. In fact," he said, a slow
smile creeping onto his face, "I should be the one de-
manding to know why you're in my father's house.''

"But you said it. I heard you say my name. Dawn,"
she said. Oh, that smile! It softened his rugged fea-

tures, made him appear younger. Crinkling little lines formed by his eyes. Eyes that were a warmer blue when he smiled.

"Dawn?" he said. "You're kidding. That's incredible. Your name is really Dawn?"

She frowned. "I've never had anyone get so charged up about it before but, yes, I'm Dawn Gilbert. I'm Elaine and Orv's niece. I brought a cherry pie over to your father, then came upstairs to pick up his mending. Are you positive you're Creed Parker?"

He chuckled, the sound seeming to rumble up from his chest, and it caused a shiver to travel down Dawn's spine.

"Creed Maxwell Parker, ma'am," he said. Ah, man, she was lovely, he thought. He was hoping to somehow find out who the mermaid had been, and here she was, standing a few feet away from him. Her last name was Gilbert, so she probably wasn't married. When he'd looked into her brown eyes, his mind had skittered to the thoughts he'd had of making love to this exquisite woman. He'd called a halt to his mental ramblings, before his body gave evidence of his desire, which would have probably scared her to death again.

"Well," she said, throwing up her hands, "it was rather startling meeting you, but welcome home."

"Thank you. I hope I didn't hurt you."

"No, but do you always wake up so violently?"

"No," he said thoughtfully. "I've been known to wake up very lovingly."

"I'll bet," she muttered, turning on her heel and starting toward the door. "See ya."

"Hey, you're not leaving, are you?" he said, following her out into the hall.

"Yes," she said, peering into Max's room. "No mending. 'Bye, Creed."

He leaned his shoulder against the wall and crossed his arms over the broad, bare expanse of his chest. When Dawn reached the top of the stairs he spoke.

"Dawn?"

"Yes?" she said, turning her head to look at him.

"When I said, 'dawn' before, I was referring to the time of day."

"Oh," she said, lifting a shoulder in a shrug. "Whatever."

"Which was when I first saw you this morning."

"You saw me this morning?" She stopped speaking as the meaning of his words sank in. "You've got a lot of nerve, Creed Parker!"

"Hey, I was on Parker land, and along comes a trespasser to the old swimming hole. I was minding my own business, then—"

"Don't you say another word!" she yelled, her cheeks crimson. "I'm going to tell your father on you! I wish you'd go back to China or wherever you came from. And take a slow boat!"

Dawn ran down the stairs, the sound of Creed's laughter following her as she dashed into the kitchen, grabbed the basket and went out the door.

Creed walked to the bedroom window and brushed back the curtain. His grin grew wider as he watched Dawn stomp toward the woods, her braids flapping against her back. She was gesturing wildly with her hand, and he had the distinct impression she was on a tirade of uncomplimentary statements against one Mr. Creed Maxwell Parker.

"Dawn," he said, letting the sound of her name roll off his tongue and echo through the room. Lovely. She

was absolutely lovely. And she was a very desirable
woman. Whew! Was she ever! She was five feet six or
seven to his six feet two, and would fit next to him like
heaven itself. Those legs. Those long, satiny legs of
Dawn's would wrap around his and... "That's all!"
he said, flopping back onto the bed, as desire rocketed through him.

He'd been too long without a woman, Creed told
himself. That was why he was overreacting to Dawn
Gilbert. Granted, she was beautiful and feminine, but
he was getting a little crazy! No, maybe not. There was
something special about her, something that had attracted him the moment he'd seen her by the swimming hole. Lust? Well, yeah, but more than that, a
strange tug at something deep within him.

"Ah, hell!" he said, drawing his hand down his
face. Why was he wasting his mental energies thinking about her? He had enough problems to deal with.
He hadn't just come home, he'd run. He'd turned his
back on it all, and run. He was empty, drained, shaken
to the core. And tired. Just so damn tired.

With a groan, he rolled over onto his stomach, gave
way to his fatigue and slept.

Dawn was still sputtering with anger when she flung
open the back door and stalked in, startling Elaine.
The mile hike through the woods had not cooled her
fury one iota.

"A sneaky snoop," she said, plunking the basket on
the table. "What he did was not the behavior becom-
ing a gentleman. And furthermore, smashing me to
smithereens on his bed wasn't very nice, either!"

"I take it you met your handsome wolf?" Elaine
said calmly, as she sat at the table shelling peas.

"Sounds like you had an interesting trip. Who is this man who has you all in a dither?"

"Creed Parker," Dawn said, collapsing in a chair.

"Creed is back? My goodness, what a surprise. Max must be so happy. Why were you in Creed's bed? Never mind, it's none of my business."

"I wasn't in it, I was on it, through no choice of my own, thank you very much. You would not believe that man's reflexes. One minute he's dead to the world, and the next he's murdering me!"

"You're exaggerating, I'm sure. You probably went barging in where you didn't belong, as per usual. That Creed is a good-looking fella, don't you think?"

"I didn't notice," Dawn said, examining her fingernails. "He was all right, I guess. You know, average."

"Oh? Then he's changed a great deal since he was here five years ago for Jane's funeral. That Creed was a handsome devil. Tall, strong, hair as black as Satan himself."

"There's a dab of gray at his temples," Dawn said absently.

"Wide shoulders, and—"

"Forget it!" Dawn said. "I'm not having this conversation. I'm going to go clean out the chicken coop." Luscious lips. Lips that would claim hers as he wrapped those arms around her and... "Chickens. 'Bye," she said, hurrying out the door.

"Welcome home, Creed," Elaine said to the empty room, as she laughed in delight. "Oh, yes, welcome home."

Creed stirred on the bed, opened his eyes, then inhaled the aroma of food that drifted up from downstairs. The gnawing emptiness in his stomach reminded him that he hadn't eaten since the day before. His eyes widened as he glanced at his watch and saw that it was nearly six o'clock. He'd slept the day away. After a shower in the bathroom at the end of the hall, he pulled on clean jeans and a black knit shirt, then walked slowly down the stairs to stand in the quiet living room.

What would he say to his father? Creed asked himself. Max had already sensed there was something wrong, had seen the weariness in his son that went beyond the need for sleep. But Max wouldn't pry, nor push. He was a man of few words, who respected the privacy of others. If Creed wished to talk, Max would listen, but the decision would be Creed's to make.

"Smells good," Creed said, entering the kitchen.

"Fried chicken," Max said. "I've learned to cook since your mother's been gone. I was beginning to wonder if you were dead to the world till morning."

"I'd have starved by then. Want some help?"

"Can you cook?"

"No," Creed said, smiling. "But I can set the table."

"Fair enough."

Creed completed his chore, then carried dishes of food to the table. The two men ate in silence for several minutes, Creed emptying his plate, then refilling it.

"This is the best meal I've had in a long time, Dad," he said finally.

"Not as good as your mother's, but I manage."

"You've said in your letters that you're doing all right here alone."

"I miss my Jane, son, but I've got a parcel full of memories to keep me company. I tend my land like I've always done, and life goes on. I like to believe that when I go to my maker, Jane will be there, and we'll be together again."

Creed shook his head. "Incredible," he said. "You have such inner peace. I envy you that."

"Why envy what you can have for yourself?"

"It's not that easy."

"Never said it was. I went through a bad spell after I lost your mother, had trouble finding a purpose, a reason to get up in the morning."

"I should have been here."

"No, Creed, you had your own life to lead. The pain was mine to deal with. I worked my way through it, and found the peace you're talking about. It's there for any man, if he wants it bad enough."

The men looked at each other for a long moment, then Creed averted his eyes and concentrated on his meal. He filled his plate for the third time.

"Gonna have room for cherry pie?" Max said, chuckling. "Elaine sent it over. The Gilberts have been mighty good to me over the years."

"Who's Dawn Gilbert?" Creed said, causing Max to look at him in surprise.

"Where did you see Dawn?"

"I saw her when . . . she came upstairs for mending or something. We talked a bit. She wasn't sure I was your son at first."

"Dawn's a joy to have around," Max said, laughing softly. "She's spread a lot of sunshine in the three years she's been at Elaine's and Orv's. Thought I mentioned her in my letters, but I guess not. Anyway, she's like a daughter to the Gilberts, makes up for them never having children."

"Yeah, but who is she? Where'd she come from? There was never a niece visiting the Gilberts when I was growing up."

"That's 'cause Orv is the black sheep of the family. Way back when, he walked away from the Gilbert family money to be a farmer. They cut him off without a penny and pretended he didn't exist. Dawn is the daughter of Orv's brother. Elaine and Orv didn't even know she existed until she showed up on their doorstep three years ago. Sorry sight she was, too."

"What do you mean?"

"It's not my place to be telling Dawn's business, Creed."

"You can't start and then stop. What do you mean, she was a sorry sight?"

"Well," Max said, frowning, "it's all behind her now, so I guess it can't hurt to tell you, long as you don't mention it to her. Dawn was married a couple of years to a rich fella her father was grooming to take over the family business. Thing was her folks thought the man was just dandy, could do no wrong, but he mistreated Dawn."

"What do you mean?"

"He beat her, son."

"Damn," Creed said, smacking his palm on the table and getting to his feet. He walked to the back door, bracing his hands on the frame and staring out the screen. A hot fury churned within him as he pictured Dawn, saw the gentle slopes of her body, the silken dew of her skin, heard the lilting sound of her laughter. That bastard! his mind roared. He'd like to get his hands on the man who'd hurt Dawn. Lord, what she must have suffered. So, she'd run. She'd come to the farm to seek solace, rebuild her life, find her peace. Everyone around him, it seemed, had found their peace.

"Want some cherry pie?" Max said quietly.

"What? Oh, yeah, sure," Creed said, returning to the table and sitting down. "I'm sorry. I guess I overreacted to what you said, but the thought of some guy abusing Dawn like that is heavy."

"Yes, but it's over, done. You saw her, Creed. She's full of life and happiness. She's twenty-six now and has her whole future ahead of her to do with as she wishes. She's been mighty content on the farm. Walked away from that high society falderal and never looked back."

"And men? Is there, well, someone special?"

"Nope. They flock to her like bees to a pretty wildflower, but she treats 'em all the same—friendly, goes here and there with 'em, but nothing serious. She says she's waiting for the cream of the crop this time 'round."

"She deserves the best," Creed said, drawing a line on the table with his spoon.

"That so?" Max said, a smile tugging at the corners of his mouth.

"Yeah, that's so," he said gruffly. "Where's this fancy pie you're raving about?"

As the pair ate huge slices of the delicious dessert, Creed glanced up at his father. How could he do it? he wondered. How could he sit there as if having his son across the table was an everyday occurrence? He had to be curious as to why Creed had suddenly arrived, how long he planned to stay. And it had to have upset him to know Creed was troubled.

"I'm not being fair to you, am I?" Creed said. "I pop up unannounced, with no explanation as to why."

"This is your home. I'm your father. You don't have to explain anything to me. Sometimes, though, it does a man good to talk, to cleanse his soul by sharing what's eating at him. I'm here, Creed. I hope you know that."

"I do," he said, his voice hushed, "and I'm grateful. But I can't tell you about it," he said, shaking his head.

"Don't rush it. You're tighter than a role of baling wire. Give yourself a chance to rest, relax. Take one day at a time for now."

"Yeah," he said. One day at a time, and each one had a dawn. Dawn. There she was again in the front of his mind. She'd been through hell, and put her life back together. And so had his father. Did he, Creed Parker, have that kind of strength? First, a man had to care about the tomorrows, and right now he didn't give a damn. Oh, yeah, he'd run, all right, to get back home. Thing was, there was nowhere he could go to escape from himself.

"Well, I've got cows to milk," Max said, getting to his feet."

"I'll do it for you."

"No, you take it easy your first day back."

"I'll clean up the kitchen then."

"Fair enough. Just put all the dishes in that fancy dishwasher you bought your mother. There's no food left to tend to."

"Guess I made a pig of myself," Creed said, smiling.

"Well, your mother used to say you're a big man, with a big appetite and a heart to match."

"I don't know about that. Mothers see what they want to see."

"Could be," Max said, nodding. "I agree with her, though. 'Course as your father, I look a bit further."

"To what?"

"The truth, or lack of it. I'll see you later," Max said, going out the door.

Creed spun in his chair and watched his father walk across the back lawn. What had he meant by that parting statement? he asked himself. How much did Max really know about Creed's life, where he'd been, what he'd done? No, there was no way he could have found out. He was sensing something was different about his son, that was all.

"I had no right to come here," Creed said under his breath. "It would break his heart if he knew the truth. But I had nowhere else to go!"

With a weary sigh, Creed got to his feet and began to clean the kitchen. When he was finished, he rewarded himself with another slice of cherry pie.

Dawn walked across the back yard and settled onto the grass, leaning her back against a tree. Conversation at dinner had centered on Creed Parker, and his image seemed determined to dance before her eyes. Aunt Elaine and Uncle Orv were obviously delighted that Creed was back, though neither could hazard a guess as to how long he'd be staying. They recounted the youthful antics of the rambunctious Creed, and laughed at the memories of the mischievous little boy.

Creed had joined the army after high school, according to Uncle Orv, then later became a diplomat in the foreign service. The Parkers apparently hadn't been disappointed that Creed hadn't stayed on the farm, Dawn mused. But knowing Max as she did, she could see that he'd want his son to be happy. But was Creed really happy? There was something about his blue eyes. They were cold, like ice chips, wary, watching for... Oh, she was being silly! She didn't even know Creed Parker.

"His body I've been introduced to," she said merrily, recalling his startling reaction after she'd woken him from sleep. And, oh, what a body. She'd felt every hard contour of him that she'd so thoroughly gawked at while he slept. Goodness, he was...male. He was also a tad frightening. Didn't diplomats go around in fancy suits attending parties? Creed had reflexes that were unbelievable. He'd sprung at her like a panther, like a man trained, conditioned to a completely different type of life. "Oh, stop it," she said aloud. "Your imagination is working overtime, Dawn Gilbert."

Oh, good grief! she thought. Creed had seen her swimming naked in the pond. Those blue eyes had swept over her. How had she measured up to the women in the fancy countries he'd been in? Oh, who cared what he thought? He'd had no right spying on her like that. Of course, she had been on Parker land, and bathing suits had been invented for a purpose, and she *had* enjoyed every minute of looking *him* over when he'd been asleep.

"That's enough time spent thinking about you, Creed Maxwell Parker," Dawn said, getting to her feet. "For all I know, you'll be gone tomorrow." Oh! she fumed, marching back to the house. Why was the thought of Creed's disappearing as quickly as he'd

come suddenly so depressing? Darn it, what was it
about that man that made it impossible to push him
very far from the center of her thoughts?

Two

———

The sound of voices woke Creed the next morning, and he bolted up on the bed, instantly wide awake. In the next moment he realized where he was and relaxed, moving slowly off the bed and walking to the window. He stood out of view due to his nakedness, and brushed back the curtain.

The acres of neat rows of vegetables had been descended upon by swarms of people carrying bushel baskets. Their voices and laughter danced across the early-morning air as the sun crept above the horizon. It was harvest time on the farm, and it was dawn.

Creed sank back onto the edge of the bed and ran his hand down his face. Dawn. He'd dreamed about her. He hadn't expected to be able to sleep at all after the hours he'd rested during the day, but he hardly remembered putting his head on the pillow.

And then he'd dreamed of Dawn. She had been in-
termixed with faces he wished to forget, had floated in
and out of familiar surroundings he never wanted to
see again. She had smiled at him, tossed the honey-
colored cascade of her hair and held out her hand,
beckoning him to come to her. Over and over he had
reached for her, but she'd been just beyond his touch.
Each time, he had been pulled back to where he didn't
want to go, had been set upon by those who haunted
him. He had struggled against their crushing weight,
calling to Dawn, then suddenly she had been gone,
disappearing into a misty fog.

"Damn!" Creed said, pushing himself to his feet.

In the shower, Creed gave himself a firm directive
regarding Dawn Gilbert. He had to quit thinking
about her! He hadn't come to the farm to become
mentally consumed by a woman. He was there to sort
through the jumbled maze in his mind, the turmoil in
his soul. He stood in a dark tunnel of self-doubt,
emptiness, and desperately needed to find himself.
There was no room for a woman in his thoughts or his
bed. Physical work was the key; the pushing of his
body until he was better equipped to take on the raging war in his head. He'd gotten himself into this living hell alone. He had to face it in the same manner—
alone. Visions of beautiful Dawn would no longer be
allowed to intrude.

Dressed in jeans and a tan T-shirt, Creed walked
down the stairs and into the kitchen.

"Creed!" Elaine said. "Glory be, it's good to see
you. Give me a hug."

Creed smiled and opened his arms to the woman
he'd known all his life.

"Hello, Elaine," he said, hugging her tightly. "It's great to see you."

"Let me look at you," she said, stepping back. "Same as ever. Too handsome for your own good. That gray in your hair just adds to your sexiness."

"Oh, yeah?" he said, chuckling. "Max didn't tell me it was harvest day. Guess you're here to cook up a storm. Mind if I have some of that coffee?"

"Help yourself," she said, moving back to the counter. "I'm just making up a batch of sandwiches. Harvest isn't like the old days, when we went from farm to farm helping each other. Those workers are all trucked in from Madison from a big commercial outfit. We feed 'em lunch, that's all. Used to be a grand time of year when everyone came together, moving from land to land, the womenfolk cooking for hours on end."

"Yeah, I remember," Creed said. "It was like a big family."

"With all you youngsters getting into mischief," Elaine said, shaking her head.

"Hey, not me. I had a permanent halo around my little head. I was a joy to raise. Never caused my folks a minute's upset."

"Drink your coffee, Creed," Elaine said, laughing, "before your nose grows out to the wall. I suppose you're hungry."

"Those ham sandwiches look good. A couple of those and the rest of this cherry pie, and I'll be all set."

"Not a farm boy's breakfast, but it'll do. Here you go."

Creed sat down at the table, ate one of the sandwiches, then started on the second.

"Orv over here?" he asked.

"Yes, he's out there supervising with Max. This outfit will be at our place tomorrow. Dawn's in the back yard making lemonade for the workers."

"Oh," he said, taking a bite of sandwich. Dawn was there? If he looked over his shoulder out the door he'd get a glimpse of her? Damn it, no! He'd settled all that twenty minutes ago. Dawn Gilbert was invisible where he was concerned.

"You met Dawn, I hear," Elaine said pleasantly.

"What? Oh, yeah, she came with the pie yesterday. Max told me she's been with you for three years."

"And every day's been a blessing. She's brought a lot of joy to our lives, as though she were our own daughter. I hate to think of her leaving us."

"Leaving?" he said, stiffening in his chair.

"Well, it's bound to happen. She's a lovely young woman who should have a family of her own. One of these days, she'll find the right man and move on."

"Not all women marry," he said, relaxing again. "If she's happy with you and Orv, likes the simple life here, she might just stay on indefinitely."

"Wouldn't be right," Elaine said firmly. "Dawn has too much love stored up inside her. She's meant to be a wife and mother."

"I understand she tried the marriage road once," Creed said, immediately feeling the knot tighten in his stomach.

"Max told you about that?"

"I pushed him a bit. You know Max, Elaine, he doesn't fill his time talking about other people's business. I just wondered how Dawn came to be here. Seems to me, she'd have every right to be down on men."

"She was at first, I suppose. She was like a frightened bird, not knowing where to go, who to trust. She reminded me of a flower, opening its petals one at a time, very carefully. Now she's a lovely blossom, full of life and happiness."

"What do her folks think about her being here?"

"We called them when she came, felt they had the right to know she was safe. They haven't contacted her since. It's hard to understand people like that. Dawn filed for divorce, took back the name Gilbert and put it all behind her. She cried her tears—many, many tears—then learned to smile again."

"Some people can do that," Creed said quietly. "My father is another one who's worked through his troubles and started over."

"You do what you have to in this life. So, tell me, Creed, how long are you going to be home? Knowing Max, he didn't ask you."

"No, he didn't," he said, picking up his dishes and carrying them to the sink. "You sure do make a great pie, Elaine."

"I know when I'm being told something is none of my business," she said, pursing her lips together.

"Elaine, I don't know how long I'll be here."

"Well, each day will be a blessing for Max. He's missed you, Creed."

"He understands that I couldn't get away. I was on the other side of the world."

"But now you're home."

"Yeah," he said, his dark brows knitting in a frown, "now I'm home. Well, I'll go hunt up Max and Orv, and find out if I can make myself useful."

"See you later."

Creed stepped out the back door and filled his lungs with the fresh morning air, again putting names to the scents that reached him. His eyes flickered over the sky, then to the woods on his right. With a defeated sigh, he slowly turned his head, knowing whom he was seeking, knowing whom he would see.

Her back was to him as she stood under a large shade tree twenty feet away. She was dressed in cut-off jeans that hugged the slender slope of her hips and curve of her buttocks. A red cotton blouse was tied under her breasts, exposing part of her back to his view. His eyes traveled the entire length of her, seeing the heavy braids, then lingering on the satiny expanse of her long legs.

His mind gave him a direct order to walk across the lawn in search of Max and Orv. The feminine lure of Dawn Gilbert bade him to journey in her direction instead.

Actually, Creed decided, it would be a good idea to see Dawn, talk to her for a few minutes. He'd met her when he was bone-weary, not really himself. Now he was rested, he would get things back in their proper perspective where she was concerned. She was a pretty woman, but not terrific enough to throw him so off balance. Strange how a man reacted when he was out on his feet. He'd get this thing settled about Dawn right now.

With a nod of his head, Creed strode across the lawn.

"'Morning," he said, as he came to where Dawn stood.

"Creed," she said, looking up at him. "Goodness, you startled me."

And then she smiled.

Ah, hell! Creed moaned silently. Her smile was like sunshine. She was beautiful. Beautiful! How could he look at her lips without thinking about kissing her? She had such soft-appearing lips, and her skin, her hair, were almost calling out for his touch. Oh, good, great, he thought in dismay. He sounded like a lunatic!

"Creed?" Dawn said, frowning slightly. "Is there something about lemonade that makes you uptight? You've got an awfully fierce expression on your face."

"What? Oh, I was just trying to figure out what you're doing."

"Making lemonade," she said. Oh, dear heaven, she thought, could he hear her heart thudding? The way that T-shirt stretched across his chest was sinful. She was going to pass out right into her tub of lemonade. Creed Parker was too much to take so early in the morning!

"Think you have enough?" he said.

"Enough what?" she said, blinking her eyes once slowly.

"Lemonade. I've never seen it made in a laundry tub before."

"Works great," she said, stirring her brew with a broom handle. "I scrubbed it to within an inch of its life. Then I multiplied the recipe a zillion times and, ta-da, enough lemonade for the harvest crew. I'll put it in those milk cans, and lug it out to the edge of the fields."

"The army could use you," he said, leaning his shoulder against the tree. "They're into cooking in quantity. I'm not sure they use broom handles, though."

Dawn laughed, the lilting reasonance causing Creed to jam his hands into the pockets of his jeans. The dream flitted before his eyes and he wanted, needed, to reach out his hand and touch her, reassure himself that she was really there. Damn it, what was wrong with him?

Dawn rested the broom handle against the edge of the tub and reached for a bucket of sugar that sat on the ground.

"I'll get it," Creed said.

In perfect synchronization it seemed, Dawn dropped to her knees as Creed hunkered down on the other side of the bucket. As her hands closed over the rim, his covered hers, then their gaze met and held.

Warm, Creed thought. Her hands were warm, soft, so delicate beneath the rough calluses of his own. She hadn't disappeared as she had in the dream. "Dawn," he said, hardly above a whisper.

The sound of her own name spoken in that husky timbre caused Dawn to draw an unsteady breath. The heat from Creed's hands was traveling up her arms, across her breasts. A wondrous yearning began deep within her and crept through her, as she was held immobile under Creed's compelling blue eyes.

Oh, what would it be like to be kissed by this man? her mind asked. Just kissed? No, more than that, much more. Creed held a promise, a gift, within the tightly muscled magnificence of his body. He exuded a blatant sexuality, a maleness, an announcement of power and strength. Never before had she been so acutely aware of the intricate differences between man and woman. Never before had she rejoiced in her own femininity. Never before had she desired anyone the way she did Creed Parker.

"What are you doing to me?" she asked, hearing the quiver in her voice.

"Dawn, ever since I saw you by the swimming hole I... No!" he said, pushing himself up, then raking his hand through his hair. "You want all of this sugar dumped in there?"

"What?"

"The sugar!" he said gruffly.

"Creed?" she said, gazing up at him questioningly.

"Dawn, don't," he said, his voice strained. "Don't look at me like that. I see desire in your eyes. And confusion, along with an almost childlike innocence and trust. For God's sake, don't trust me!"

"I'm not a child!"

"Damn it, lady, do you think I don't know that? I ache with the want of you, Dawn Gilbert, and I don't intend to do a damn thing about it. I don't need this kind of trouble. I'm not going to bed with you!"

"Well, who in the hell asked you to?" she yelled, scrambling to her feet. "You're taking a lot for granted here, Mr. Parker. I have never in my life met a man with such an overblown ego. Maybe your fancy foreign females drool all over your tight T-shirts and sexy jeans, but I'm totally unimpressed. I wouldn't sleep with you if you were the last—"

"That's it!" he grated, hauling her to him by the upper arms and bringing his mouth down hard onto hers.

In the next instant the kiss gentled into a soft sensuous embrace, as Creed gathered Dawn to the hard wall of his chest, his arms folding around her in a protective embrace. Of their own volition it seemed, her hands crept upward to link behind his neck, her fingers inching into the thick, night-darkness of his hair. She parted her lips to receive his questing tongue, which dueled, danced, flickered over and around hers.

Creed had the irrational thought that he was drowning. He was being swept away on a tide of passion that he had no wish to escape from. The taste, the feel, the aroma of the woman in his arms was sweet torture, agony and ecstasy, heaven and hell. An eternity had passed from the moment he had seen Dawn until now, until this kiss.

A soft moan penetrated the hazy mist of Dawn's mind, and a sense of panic washed over her as she realized she didn't know if the passion-laden sound had come from her or Creed. Dear heaven, what were they doing?

"Creed!" she gasped, pressing her hands against his chest.

He lifted his head and looked down at her, his eyes a smoky blue, sending a readable message of desire. With a shuddering breath, he trailed his hands down her arms, then stepped back, his gaze never leaving hers. A crackling, sensual tension hung in the air, nearly palpable in its intensity.

"If I said I was sorry," Creed said, his voice gritty, "I'd be lying."

"Creed, I don't want any apologies."

"Hear me out," he said, raising his hand, then shoving both into his back pockets. "Something is happening here, with us, that I don't understand. I've never experienced anything like it before. It could be old-fashioned lust, I suppose, but I have a feeling it might be a hell of a lot more than that. Thing is, Dawn, whatever it is, I'm walking away from it."

"Why?"

"Why?" he said, with a bitter-sounding laugh. "Because you deserve better than this, than me."

"You don't even know me, let alone what I deserve."

"I know you. Dawn, I told you not to trust me, and I meant it. Just because I'm Max's son doesn't guarantee that I'm anything like him. Max is a warm, giving, loving human being."

"And you, Creed? What—who are you?" she said, wrapping her hands around her elbows.

"I wish to God I knew," he said, his voice flat.

And then she saw it.

The pain.

Deep in the blue pools of Creed Parker's eyes, Dawn saw a haunting depth of anguish. Her breath caught in her throat, and she lifted her hand toward him before she realized she had moved.

"No!" he said, then turned and strode away in the direction of the barn.

Dawn pressed her fingertips to her lips, and blinked back her sudden tears. She wanted to run after Creed, comfort him, soothe away his pain, chase into oblivion the demons that stalked him. He *was* a warm, giving, loving human being. He was! His kiss had been sensuous, his strength tempered with infinite gentleness. She had felt his muscles tremble as he strove for control as he'd held her, so safely, so protectively, in his arms.

What had happened to Creed? Dawn mused, absently pouring the sugar into the tub. What had caused the happy, mischievous little boy to become a haunted man? Had he been hurt by a woman, by love? She had known the pain of that kind of betrayal, and hers had been accompanied by physical abuse as well. No, she didn't think it was a woman. She just didn't think so. The turmoil Creed was suffering seemed to be directed at himself *from* himself. She wanted desperately to help him, but how?

"Oh, my," she said, sighing deeply, "I think I'd better just concentrate on my lemonade."

Creed headed around the side of the barn, avoiding contact with Max and Orv. Sweat ran down his back and his heart thundered in his chest. His eyes darted in all directions, wary, watching for any signs or clue that he was in danger. Every muscle in his body was tensed, coiled, ready.

"No!" he said. "No, I'm home. Home!"

He drew in a shuddering breath, then leaned against the side of the barn, resting his head on the weather-beaten wood, and closing his eyes. His heartbeat quieted. The smells of the farm inched into his senses, the sounds of his youth, of a time past. A time of inner peace.

He'd felt it, that peace, when he'd been holding Dawn Gilbert. Everything had faded into oblivion but her—the sweetness of her mouth, her special feminine aroma, the softness of her body pressed to his. Dawn had replaced the ugliness within him with the very essence of herself. He'd taken from her, and given nothing in return.

"Stay away from her, Parker," he said aloud, pushing himself away from the barn. He'd tried to tell her that she deserved better than what he was. But then she'd pressed him for an answer as to who *was* Creed Maxwell Parker. The emptiness, the black void within him had hit him like a ton of bricks. So he'd

run again. Like a scared kid, he lit out to hide behind
the barn. "Damn," he said, shaking his head.

Creed walked slowly around the side of the building, then uttered a colorful expletive at what he saw.
Dawn was pulling an obviously heavy milk can
through the thick grass in the direction of the fields.
Creed took off toward her at full speed.

"Damn it, Dawn!" he said, when he reached her.

"Damn it, Creed!" she yelled. "Quit sneaking up
on me every two minutes."

"That can is too heavy for you!"

"Says who?" she said, releasing her hold and placing her hands on her hips.

"Me!" he said, moving in front of the can.

"Oh, is that so! Well, guess what, Mr. Macho, I got
along perfectly fine around here before you showed
up. I'm very capable of hauling this milk can from
here to there. Now move out of my way!"

"No!" he said, crossing his arms over his chest.

"I'm warning you, Parker!"

"Don't push me, Gilbert!"

"And don't you dare holler at me. I thought diplomats were diplomatic! You probably screamed your
way around the world. Get away from my milk can!
This is the United States of America, and I have my
rights! I—"

"You're done," he said, and in the next instant he
picked Dawn up and flung her over his shoulder, circling her legs tightly with his arms. "Cute tush," he
said, giving it a friendly pat.

"Put me down!" Dawn shrieked, whopping Creed's
back with her fists.

His throaty chuckle only infuriated her more, as he set off across the grass in the direction of Max and Orv.

"Creed Maxwell Parker, put me down!"

The two older men looked up in surprise as Creed and his cargo descended on them.

"Hello, Orv," Creed said calmly. "Long time no see."

"The blood is running to my head!" Dawn said. "My teeth are falling out!"

"Mighty good to have you home, Creed," Orv said.

"Help! Uncle Orv! Max! Help!"

"What do you think of our fancy harvest crew, son?" Max said.

"They sure work fast," Creed said, nodding. "Seems like a real efficient outfit. I understand they're doing your crops tomorrow, Orv."

"Yep."

"I'm going to strangle this barbarian with my bare hands!" Dawn said, giving Creed a solid whack on the rear.

"Out for a stroll?" Orv said, his shoulders shaking with laughter.

"No," Creed said slowly. "I need you two to baby-sit this brat so I can tote those milk cans down to the field."

"Aaak!" Dawn screamed. "Don't you touch my milk cans!"

Dawn grabbed one of her flying braids in her hand, and in the next instant, pulled Creed's T-shirt free of his jeans. She danced the end of the silky hair across his bare tanned back and giggled in delight as she saw the muscles jump.

"Dawn!" Creed said. "That tickles. Get out of my pants!"

She wiggled the braid with vigor.

"Oh, man!" Creed said, laughter rumbling up from his chest.

"Wanna place any bets?" Max said to Orv.

"Nope. I'd say it's a pretty even match."

"Think you're right," Max said, his blue eyes alive with merriment.

"Dawn! Cut it out!"

"Put me down!"

"I give up," Creed said, swinging her off his shoulder and setting her on her feet. "You're a wicked woman."

"Don't speak to me, Parker," she said, stomping away. "I'm going to go wash out my laundry tub."

"Don't go near my milk cans," he called after her.

"Oh, Lordy, you've got hell to pay now, boy," Orv said, laughing heartily. "She's got a temper on her, our Dawn."

"Don't worry about a thing," Creed said, striding off toward the milk can.

"Wouldn't have missed that for the world," Max said.

Creed carried the milk can to the edge of the field, then retrieved the other from beneath the tree. Dawn was hosing out the laundry tub, and ignored Creed as he picked up the second can. Her stormy expression caused him to whoop with laughter, and she gritted her teeth. His mission accomplished, Creed strolled back to the tree and watched as Dawn continued to spray the tub.

"I might mention," he said, "that if you have any ideas about dousing me with that hose, you'd do well to reconsider your diabolical plan."

"Oh, now, Creed," she said, ever so sweetly, "do you actually think I would do something like that? Me?"

"It crossed my mind," he said, chuckling.

They looked at each other, then burst into laughter, the engaging sounds mingling together in the summer air. Then Creed's expression grew serious, and he reached out to trail his thumb over the smooth skin of her cheek.

"You're quite a woman, Dawn Gilbert," he said, his voice low.

"You make a great caveman," she said, a breathlessness to her voice. Tearing her gaze from his, she continued, "I guess this is clean. I'll put it back in the barn."

Dawn walked over to shut off the water, then turned to see Creed holding the laundry tub in one hand.

"Here we go again," she said.

"Let's call a truce," he said, smiling at her. "I'll tote it, you show me where you want it put."

"Okay," she said, throwing up her hands. "I know when I'm licked."

They walked in silence for a few moments before Creed spoke.

"You're happy here with Elaine and Orv, aren't you?" he said, more as a statement than a question.

"Yes, very happy. It's totally different from the way I was raised. I was a very spoiled little rich girl."

"It's hard to imagine you like that."

"Oh, I was a classic case. Finest clothes, best schools and absolutely no sense of identity, who I was.

I followed my parents' rules to the letter, never questioned a thing."

"Including their choice of a husband for you?"

Dawn looked up at him in surprise. "You know about that?"

"I asked because I was interested in who you were, how you came to be here. I'm sorry for prying into your business, but I really wanted to know more about you."

"It doesn't matter," she said, as they entered the barn. "It was a long time ago. I feel as though it happened to someone else. The laundry tub goes over there in the corner."

Creed put the tub in place, then returned to the center of the barn where Dawn stood.

"But why the farm? Why did you come to the Gilberts'?"

"I don't know. I'd heard my parents talking about Uncle Orv once, and tucked it in the back of my mind, I guess. When I left Chicago—no, ran from there—I came here. Elaine and Orv took me in, and have given me so much love. This has been the happiest three years of my life."

"How did you do it? Forget the nightmare you'd been through."

"I'll never really forget it, Creed. In fact, it's important that I remember in a detached sort of way, so I never take for granted how much I have now. It took me months to really get over what had happened. And during those months, I cried. The tears were always close to the surface, ready to spill over. Aunt Elaine told me to cry whenever I felt the need, and I did. My tears were a cleansing thing, just like when a soft spring rain comes to the farm. And then? I stopped

crying, because it was over, finished, and it was time
to start fresh.''

"Incredible," Creed said, shaking his head.

"Men have been taught that they shouldn't cry
when they're hurting, and that's wrong. They go out
and get drunk, or punch somebody in the nose, but it
doesn't solve a thing. There's no shame in showing
emotions, Creed. Tears can wash away a lot of pain."

He looked down at her, a deep frown on his face.
"Tears aren't always the answer," he said.

"But many times they are," she said, her voice
hushed.

The dim light of the barn cast flickering shadows
over Creed's face as Dawn gazed up at him, searching, seeking some clue as to what he was thinking. She
could not clearly see the message in his blue eyes, as he
stood statue still before her. It wasn't until he exhaled
a rush of air that she realized he had been nearly
holding his breath as he listened to her softly spoken
words.

"Dawn," he said, then opened his arms to her.

With no hesitation she moved into his embrace, relishing the strength of his muscle-corded arms that
folded around her, savoring his aroma, the heat
emanating from his body, as she rested her head on the
hard wall of his chest.

And then he held her.

Simply held her.

Dawn's eyes drifted shut, and a soft sigh of contentment whispered from her lips as she and Creed
stood perfectly still, close, nestled against each other
in a seemingly endless stretch of time. All sounds and
smells disappeared into a hazy mist. For Dawn, there
was only Creed.

Then slowly, tiny sensations of desire began to stir within her, kindling the ember of need to a rambling fire that licked throughout her. She trembled in Creed's arms, and he pulled her closer, his own arousal evident as he fit her more tightly to the rugged contours of his frame. In an unspoken message, sent and received, she lifted her head as he lowered his, and their lips met, parted, tongues joining, as passions soared.

She circled his neck with her arms, pressing her mouth harder, harder, onto his. Her heart beat wildly against her ribs, as their labored breathing echoed in the quiet building. Creed's hands slid up to cup the sides of her breasts, his thumbs inching inward, stroking, bringing the buds to taut, throbbing awareness. The kiss grew more frenzied, urgent. He groaned deep in his chest, his muscles trembling as he strove for control.

"Dawn," he said, moving his hands to her waist.

"Oh, Creed," she said, taking a shuddering breath. "You make me feel so..."

"I know. I feel the same way. It's different from anything I've ever felt. I want you, Dawn. I want to make love to you so much, so very much."

"And I want you to make love to me," she said quietly, looking directly into his eyes. "I've never said that to a man before. I know I was married, but it's as though this is the first time for me. I do want you."

He cupped her face in his hands and gazed at her, a gentle smile on his face.

"Dawn's gift," he said. "That's you. My gift from the dawn. I desire you like no woman before. But until I work through some things I have to tackle, I can't make love to you. I just can't. I'm not rejecting you, I'm protecting you, from me."

"But . . ."

"Yeah, I know you can take care of yourself, make your own decisions. So, okay, I'll rephrase it. This isn't the right time for *me*. Dawn, I may never get myself squared away. It may be too late for me. When I hold you, kiss you, you're all that matters. But when I step back I have to face who, what I am, mixed up with the fact that I don't know who I am at all." He stopped speaking and moved away, raking a restless hand through his hair.

"I don't understand. Creed, what happened to you? What are you running from?"

"Myself," he said, his voice hushed. "I'm running from myself, which I'm discovering is impossible. I shouldn't have come home, but I had nowhere else to go. My father senses that I'm troubled, but I just can't tell him why."

"And me? Will you talk to me? I'll listen, Creed, you know I will."

"No. The problems are mine to solve."

"Do you think it's a sign of weakness to share, to ask for help? I don't think I would have survived if it hadn't been for Elaine and Orv. Whatever it is, Creed, you don't have to suffer through it alone. I'm here. I'll—"

"No!" he said sharply.

"All right. I won't try to push myself on you. But please, Creed, talk to Max. You said yourself that he realizes something is wrong. If I can see the pain in your eyes, then Max can see it, too. Go to your father."

"And say what?" he asked, his chest heaving. "That somewhere along the line I misplaced his son, lost his precious boy halfway around the world? Tell him...that it was all a pack of lies? The letters. All those letters were a bunch of bull, don't you understand? How proud my folks were of their son the foreign diplomat. Pages and pages I wrote about fancy parties, homes, important people I'd met, and none of it was true!"

"My God," she whispered.

"Is that what you want me to tell Max? I can't. I won't break that man's heart. He lost his wife. I can't tell him the son he knew is gone, too!"

"You're not gone! You're standing here. You're home!"

"No, Dawn," he said, his voice suddenly low and flat. "The body, the shell is here, but Creed Maxwell Parker no longer exists. There's nothing left inside of me. I'm empty, drained, living in a black tunnel of hell. I have nothing to offer you, or Max, or anyone. I'd only take."

An amalgam of emotions assaulted Dawn as she stared at Creed—emotions of helplessness, frustration, of wanting to bring comfort to this man who was suffering but who would accept no assistance. An ache seemed to settle over her heart, a heavy weight that caused an actual physical discomfort.

If only he would cry, she thought. She'd hold him so close, hold him while he wept because... Oh, dear heaven, no! She wasn't falling in love with Creed, was she? Whatever this jumble in her heart and mind was, surely it couldn't be love!

Three

Dawn?" Creed said. "Are you all right?"

"What?" she asked. "Oh yes, I'm fine."

"I realize that all I've done is talk in circles, but it's the best I can do for now."

"I understand. I didn't mean to pry," she said, managing a weak smile. Lies? All those letters to Max hadn't held a word of truth? If Creed wasn't a foreign diplomat, then what was he? *Who* was he? Dear heaven, what had he done to be filled with such pain?

"I've frightened you, haven't I?" he said, raking his hand through his hair. "I can see it in your eyes. You look just like you did when I jumped you in my bedroom yesterday. I'm sorry, Dawn. I've said more to you about myself than I should have. I had no intention of dragging you into this, upsetting you. I don't suppose you could just forget what I said about those letters I wrote to Max?"

"Forget? No, Creed," she said, shaking her head, "that's impossible. But you have my word that I won't tell anyone."

"I appreciate that. Look, I'm going to hunt up some tools and see if I can fix the front steps of the house."

"All right. I'll go see if Elaine needs any help with the food for the harvest crew."

"Aren't you going to thank me for carrying those milk cans to the field for you?" he said, smiling at her.

Dawn burst into laughter. "No, I am not, Mr. Parker! Your display of machismo was totally unimpressive."

"Well, shucks, I tried. You got an interesting ride out of the deal, you know. You're the prettiest, softest sack of potatoes I've ever toted over my shoulder."

And what a gorgeous shoulder it was, Dawn mused. "I could have lived without it," she said, smiling. His back was tan, taut, had actually rippled when she'd flicked her braid over his smooth skin. Beautiful. "Well, I'll see you later!"

"Dawn?"

"Yes?"

"Thanks."

Their eyes met in a steady gaze, and Dawn instantly felt the tingle of desire begin deep within her. A part of her mind registered a flash of anger that she was so susceptible to Creed's blatant sexuality, his vibrant masculinity. But another section of her thoughts rejoiced in the new, strange, wondrous sensations he evoked throughout her. She felt alive as never before, so aware of her own femininity.

She had responded to Creed's kiss and touch with an abandon that both shocked and pleased her. She'd come alive, really alive, in the circle of his arms. Had she actually offered herself to this man? She, Dawn Gilbert, who gave chaste kisses at her front door, had boldly told Creed she wanted him to make love to her? Yes, she'd done it, all right.

Question was, would she have gone through with it? Made love with him? Or had she subconsciously known there were people tromping around outside the barn, that she and Creed were not really alone? Good grief, why didn't she know herself better than this? Since meeting Creed Parker a facet of her had surfaced that she'd been unaware even existed! What was this man doing to her?

Creed suddenly cleared his throat and averted his eyes from Dawn's, breaking the sensual spell that had once again woven itself around them like silken threads.

"I'll get started on the steps," he said.

"Okay. 'Bye for now," Dawn said, hearing the slight tremor in her voice.

She hurried out of the barn, then slowed as she walked toward the house. The summer sun caressed her skin and she took a deep breath, feeling as though she had returned to familiar surroundings from an unknown place. And, in a way, it was true. Creed had swept her away on a tide of passion, as well as evoking within her temptestuous emotions of physical wanting, needing, and an urge to help and comfort him. Her calm, pleasant existence was being turned topsy-turvy due to the arrival of Creed Maxwell Parker.

When Dawn entered the kitchen, Elaine immediately burst into laughter.

"Well, thanks," Dawn said. "I didn't know I was so funny looking."

"I have never in my born days seen such goings-on out a kitchen window," Elaine said. "Creed kissed you one minute, and the next? He threw you over his shoulder and marched away. I was laughing so hard, I had tears running down my cheeks. Mercy, the two of you together are something."

"You were watching out the window?" Dawn said, feeling the warmth of a blush on her cheeks.

"Certainly. It was more fun than I've had in ages. I was disappointed when you went into the barn. Couldn't see a thing from here."

"For Pete's sake," Dawn said.

"That Creed is quite a man. I remember when he was in high school, and the girls used to swarm all over him. I imagine he's had his share of women while he's been flitting around the world."

"Am I supposed to be getting a message here?" Dawn said, frowning.

"Oh, honey," Elaine said, sighing, "I don't know what to say. My heart was singing with joy when I saw Creed kissing you. But then, well, I realized I still think of him as the Creed I watched grow from a boy to be such a handsome man. Truth is, he's been away a long time, could very well be someone I don't know at all. There's just something about him.... Well, I've said enough."

"What do you mean, there's something about him?"

"His eyes, honey. He used to have warm, laughing eyes, blue as the sky, like Max's. But now? There's something different about Creed's eyes, a winter chill, icy, cold. It's as though the life has gone out of him. I guess I'm not making much sense."

"Yes, you are," Dawn said quietly.

"I love that boy like he was my own, but I love you, too, Dawn. Tread softly until you're sure you know what you're doing. Remember, Creed hasn't said one word about being home to stay. He's vague on the subject, says he isn't sure how long he'll be here. I don't want you hurt, Dawn. All right, now you can tell me to mind my own business."

"I love you, Aunt Elaine," Dawn said, kissing her on the cheek. "Don't worry about me. I'm not the naive child I was when I arrived on your doorstep three years ago. I'm all grown-up now, know who I am, and what I'm doing. I appreciate your concern, but it really isn't necessary." Oh, ha! she thought. What a bunch of blarney! Nice spiel, and used to be true. Right up until she'd seen the beautiful bum sleeping in the green room. "What can I do to help you with the food?"

Dawn chatted with her aunt as they prepared lunch for the harvest crew, striving for a lightness to her voice, a relaxed air of normalcy. In actuality, she was shaken to the core, as the endless questions about Creed screamed in her mind. And with them came the unknowns about herself.

At noon, Max and Orv carried the trays of sandwiches, fruit and pies to the field. Elaine announced she'd serve lunch in the kitchen in exactly ten minutes, and instructed Dawn to find Creed. Dawn walked through the house to the front door, then stopped, her breath catching in her throat as she saw him.

He had removed his T-shirt and his broad, tanned
back glistened with perspiration. The faded jeans rode
low on his hips as he bent over, sawing a section of
wood he had propped on a crate. The muscles in his
back, shoulders and arms bunched and moved with
the steady rhythm of the saw.

There she stood, Dawn thought ruefully, gawking
at Creed Parker again. She was either thinking about
him, leaping into his arms or staring at him like a love-
struck teenager. Love-struck? No! She absolutely,
positively was *not* falling in love with this man. In the
first place, love didn't happen this quickly. Did it? No.
Physical attraction? Yes. But love? Certainly not.

And secondly, she mentally continued, since she was
basically a nice person, she was simply concerned because Creed was troubled. A great deal of her preoc-
cupation with him could be chalked up to her maternal
instincts. Oh, really? She hadn't felt like his mother
when he'd been kissing her, that was for sure! And
when he pinned her in place with those icy blue eyes of
his? She was a goner. She was also going to wear out
her brain if she didn't take time off from the jumble
in her mind. Enough was enough.

Dawn pushed opened the door, which creaked on its
hinges, and in the next instant gasped in shock. At the
movement behind him, Creed dropped the saw, then
wheeled around, crouching low as one arm shot out in
front of him, his other hand flying to the back of the
waistband of his jeans. It had been executed in the
quick, smooth, powerful motion of one conditioned,
highly trained, moving with a sixth sense. And Dawn
saw it all.

Creed straightened his stance as she stepped out
onto the porch. He planted his hands on his hips and

stared up at the sky, taking a long, weary-sounding
breath before he looked at her again. She stood statue
still, eyes wide, her heart racing beneath her breast.

"Creed?" she said, her voice hushed. "You were
reaching for a gun, weren't you?"

"Let it go, Dawn," he said, his voice low, flat.

"No! I could tell that what you just did was as natural to you as breathing. It's just like what happened
in your room yesterday. Why do you have reflexes like
that? Why would you automatically go for a gun when
you heard a noise behind you? Why, Creed?"

"Damn it," he roared, "give it a rest! I told you I
had no intention of discussing my personal life with
you, or anyone else, and I meant it! I can't erase what
you just saw, but I sure as hell don't owe you an explanation for it!"

"No. No, of course, you don't," she said, clasping
her trembling hands behind her. "It's none of my
business."

"Ah, man," he said, running his hand down his
face.

"I, uh, just came to tell you that lunch is ready,"
she said, turning toward the door.

"Dawn, wait."

"Yes?" she said, facing him again.

"Give me some time to sort all this through, okay?
I know it's not fair to shut you out one minute, then
pull you into my arms the next. And, oh, yes, Dawn
Gilbert, I do want you in my arms. Could you trust
me. No, forget that. Why should you trust me?"

But she did! Dawn realized. She had no reason to,
but she did trust Creed. She didn't know who or what
he was, but at that moment it didn't matter. He was
asking for time and trust, and she would give it to him.

Why? She didn't know that, either. She certainly didn't know a heck of a lot!

"Fair enough, Creed," she said. "I won't push you for any answers."

"Fair enough?" he said, smiling slightly. "You sound like Max."

"Yes, I guess I do. He's an important part of my life, just like Elaine and Orv are. You're coming in for lunch, aren't you?"

"Yeah, I'll wash up, put my shirt on and be right there. Am I asking too much, Dawn? You're giving me time, trust, keeping my secrets from Max. Is it too much?"

"No, Creed, it's not. I don't know why, but it's not."

They stared at each other for a long moment, then Creed nodded. Dawn walked slowly into the house.

Lunch proved to be a jovial affair, with everyone giving a slightly different slant to the tale of Dawn, Creed and the milk cans. Laughter echoed in the Parker kitchen, and Dawn decided she had never seen Max look happier.

"Peach, apple or cherry pie?" Elaine said finally.

"Yes," Creed said.

"Land's sake," Elaine said, "he's got a hollow leg."

"I bet good farm cooking tastes dandy after those fancy foreign foods you've been eating, Creed," Orv said. "'Course, there's no gold-edged plates to eat off of like you diplomats are used to."

Dawn looked up quickly at Creed, but he appeared calm and relaxed.

"I'll rough it," he said, smiling.

"You sure rubbed elbows with important people," Elaine said, putting the dessert on the table. "Did you ever wear a tuxedo with a ruffled shirt?"

"Yes," Creed said, taking a big bite of peach pie.

"Did the women have beautiful gowns and elaborate hairstyles?" Elaine asked.

"Everyone decked out in their finery for embassy affairs," he said. "The waiters wore white gloves, and served champagne in crystal glasses on silver trays. Classy."

"Mercy, imagine that," Elaine said wistfully.

Lies, Dawn thought. It was all lies! Creed wasn't a diplomat! How easily the fabrications flowed off his tongue, how at ease he was spinning his fantasies, creating stories of the glamorous life he had led. But where had he really been, and what had he been doing? With a gun.

"Dawn?" Elaine said.

"What? Oh, I'm sorry. I was daydreaming."

"I asked you if you wanted some pie."

"No, thank you. I'll help you clean up here, then I'd better get home and tend to my babies."

Creed's fork halted halfway to his mouth. "I beg your pardon?" he said.

"Cute little buggers," Max said. "Dawn's babies are real dolls. Win your heart in a minute."

"I didn't realize you had . . ." Creed started. "You left your babies alone?"

"Well, I can't tote them everywhere I go," Dawn said, picking up one braid and studying the end of it. "I have a right to a little freedom, you know."

Creed scowled.

Max, Elaine and Orv dissolved in a laughing fit.

Dawn blew on the end of her braid with an expression of innocence on her face.

"Okay," Creed said, a slow grin tugging at his lips. "I know when I've been had. What's the deal, the con?"

"To what are you referring, sir?" Dawn asked, raising her eyebrows.

"Your babies," he said, grinning at her.

"Oh, them! Little dolls, just like Max said. I have a reputation all the way to Madison for making beautiful babies. Cute ones, too."

"I'd like a picture of your face, Creed," Max said, blue eyes dancing. "Close your mouth before you catch flies."

"He had it coming for the milk cans," Dawn said. "All right, Creed Parker, I will now take pity on you, since you're slightly outnumbered. Dawn's Dolls is my business. I sew handmade baby dolls with complete wardrobes, and sell them in shops in Madison."

"No kidding?" Creed said. "I'm impressed. You'll have to show me your babies."

"Be glad to," she said. "They're sweet."

"Yeah, real dolls," he said, laughing. "You had me going there for a minute."

"Can't you picture Dawn as a mother?" Elaine said.

"I most certainly can," Creed said, looking directly at Dawn. "Oh, yes, I can see Dawn with a child. It was the part about leaving them over there alone that threw me. She'd never do that. Right, Dawn?"

"No. No, of course, I wouldn't," she said, meeting his gaze. He could see her with a child? No man had ever said that about her before. Most saw her as a pretty decoration, an object to show off on their arm.

What kind of father would Creed make? "Time to clean up," she said, getting to her feet. "And, Creed? Be sure and hose out *your* milk cans very thoroughly when you bring them up from the field. That lemonade is sticky stuff."

Max, Elaine and Orv started laughing again.

Creed went back to scowling.

The meal completed, everyone dispersed. Creed tugged on one of Dawn's braids as he passed her, and told Elaine she made the best pies in the state of Wisconsin.

"It's good to have him home," Elaine said to Dawn. "There was laughter in this house today, just like when Jane was alive."

"How did she die?"

"Pneumonia. She always was a frail little thing, and Max and Creed used to take such good care of her. She caught cold that winter and, well, we lost her. Max was beside himself with grief."

"Did Creed come home when he heard his mother was ill?"

"It was all rather confusing. Jane was in the hospital in Madison, and Max was phoning the State Department over and over, asking them to get a message to Creed. They kept telling Max someone would call and let Max know when Creed could get here. You would have thought they'd have given Max the number of Creed's fancy embassy or whatever it was. Anyway, Max never heard a word, and he'd call again. But Jane died before Creed got home. He arrived the morning of the funeral."

"I see," Dawn said quietly.

"Creed could only stay a week. He came to me and Orv and asked us to take care of his father, said he was very worried about him. 'Course, we were planning on watching over Max, anyway. Oh, my heart did ache for Creed. He never had a chance to say goodbye to his mother, his father was in terrible shape and he had to pack up and go."

Go where? Dawn wondered. *To do what?* Hadn't Max ever questioned why it had been so difficult to locate someone as visible as a diplomat for the United States government? No, not dear, sweet Max. Trusting Max, who took everything at face value and passed no censure.

"Creed made plans to visit several times in the past five years," Elaine went on, "but something always kept him from getting home. Now, here he is without a word beforehand saying he was coming. I guess working for the government is very unpredictable. 'Course, he wrote all the time, even phoned now and then. I'm sure you can see how much having him here means to Max. I just wish..."

"Wish what, Aunt Elaine?"

"That I didn't sense such a change in Creed, see the difference in that boy's eyes. Maybe I'm being foolish, but I think he's uneasy about something, troubled. Max must have noticed, but he'd never say a word to Creed. No, Creed would have to go to his father and bring it all out in the open. I just can't help but worry about Creed, though. And I worry about you, too."

"You worry about everyone, and I love you for it," Dawn said. "Look, perhaps Creed is just tired, needs a vacation. I'm sure that being a diplomat is a very high-pressure career. Maybe you're just imagining some of the distress you sense in him.''

''Maybe,'' Elaine said, nodding. ''I hope so. Well, let's get these pies covered. That Creed sure made a dent in each one. That boy knows how to eat!''

And she was learning how to lie, Dawn thought dismally.

After the kitchen was cleaned, Elaine said she'd check if the harvest crew had gotten enough to eat.

''I'll see you at home,'' Dawn said, then turned as loud hammering came from the direction of the living room.

''He'll bring the roof down,'' Elaine said, going out the back door.

Dawn wandered into the living room, purposely clearing her throat as she entered to warn Creed of her arrival. She did not, she decided, wish to witness another display of his razor-sharp reflexes.

'''Lo,'' Creed said, glancing at her over his shoulder.

''Goodness, you're busy.''

''Just tightening up this banister. It's nice to know I haven't lost my touch with a hammer and saw.''

And his touch with a gun? Dawn asked in her mind. She had to stop thinking about it. The whole thing was beginning to drive her crazy!

''So,'' Creed said, ''are you off to tend to your babies?''

''Yes,'' she said, smiling, ''duty calls.''

''Dawn's Dolls. How did you get started on such an unusual endeavor?''

''By accident, really. When I came to Aunt Elaine and Uncle Orv's, I was a lost soul, if you will. I won't go into all the boring details, but I had no self-esteem, into a workroom, and I go to it. It's very rewarding, not just financially, but..."

"I understand, and I think it's terrific. I admire you, Dawn, for the way you've gotten a handle on your life, found yourself, your direction."

"Thank you. I owe a great deal to the love and support I got from Elaine and Orv. Max, too. He's been wonderful to me. I insist on paying room and board to Elaine and Orv."

"Uh-oh."

"Tell me about it. Elaine sputters every month when I give her the money, then stuffs it in the cookie jar. I don't think she's touched a penny of it in the past couple of years."

"She loves you like a daughter. Elaine wouldn't feel right taking money from her own family."

"Well, I give it to her anyway. It makes me feel better, but there's really no way to repay someone for their love."

"Except by loving them in return," Creed said quietly, turning to face her.

"Have you ever been in love?

"With a woman? No."

"But there's been a lot of women in your life."

"There has?" he said, smiling at her.

"Oh, come on, Creed. You're a good-looking man, and I'm sure women have been chasing you for years. Why am I standing here puffing up your ego?"

"Okay, so I've had my share of women. But I've never been in love. Have you?"

"No."

"Not even with your husband when you first married him?"

"No. The Dawn Gilbert who married him is someone I no longer know. When I marry again, I'll be in
love, absolutely bonkers for the guy," she said,
laughing.

"He'll be a lucky man," Creed said, his voice low.
Dawn being held, kissed, touched, made love to, by
someone other than himself? Dawn growing big with
another man's child? Damn it, he didn't like the sound
of that. Not one little bit! Oh, yeah? Where did he get
off having such possessive thoughts about her?

"You certainly switch moods fast," Dawn said.
"You look like you're about to punch somebody in the
nose."

"What? Oh, I was just thinking about something.
So, where are you going to find this dreamboat of
yours?"

"Around," she said breezily.

"Change the subject," he said, frowning deeply.

"Why?"

"Because I'm the guy you said you wanted to make
love with!" he said, none too quietly. Dawn jumped
in surprise. "I don't want to stand here discussing the
jerk you're going to marry!"

"He's not a jerk! Oh, this is stupid! He doesn't even
exist!"

"Good. Keep it that way," he said gruffly, slam-
ming the tools back into the box.

Dawn opened her mouth with every intention of
giving Creed Parker a piece of her mind, then shut it
again. Goodness! she thought, how possessive he
sounded.

"Forget I said that," Creed said. "I don't have any
claim on you."

Oh, darn, Dawn thought.

"Yes, damn it, I do!" he roared in the next instant.
"You respond to my kiss, my touch. There's something happening between us, Dawn, and it's not just
lust. I desire you, but it's more than that. I... Ah, hell,
forget it."

"Again? Would you kindly make up your mind? I
can't keep up with you. It's like having a conversation with a Ping-Pong ball."

Creed glared at her, then rested his arm on the end
of the banister as he ran his other hand over the back
of his neck. A slow smile inched onto his lips, then
widened into a grin.

"I've been called a lot of things in my day," he said,
"but never a Ping-Pong ball."

Dawn burst into laughter. "Oh, Creed," she said,
"you and I, together, are exhausting."

"You and I, together," he said, pushing off the
banister and closing the distance between them, "are
a glimpse of heaven itself." He cupped her face in his
large hands. "When I kiss you, Dawn, I don't want to
stop. My mind goes further, sees us making love, be-
coming one. Oh, yes, there is something very special
happening between us."

"Creed, I can feel it, too."

"Thing is, I can't promise you that I'll find my answers, my inner peace. I just don't know. Dawn, I
don't want to hurt you, but I could, don't you see? If
I find no escape from my dark tunnel, I'll have nothing to offer you. Nothing. If you tell me to stay away
from you, I'll understand, and I won't touch you
again."

Not touch her again? Dawn's mind echoed. Not kiss
her, hold her, make her feel alive, feminine, filled with
wondrous sensations? Walk away from Creed as

though his emergence into her life had held no signif-
icance, had been nothing more than a fleeting fancy?
No! It was too late for that! If he left her now, this
very minute, she would miss him, want to see his
smile, want to be gathered into the strong circle of his
arms, and press her lips to his.

He held the power to shatter her into a million
pieces, should he disappear as quickly as he had come,
for he had already staked an unnamed claim on her.
She should order him out of her life while she still
possessed a modicum of reasoning. But she couldn't,
and she knew it. She was probably a breath away from
falling in love with this man, who had frightening secrets and inner demons to fight. In battles there were
winners and losers, the victors and those defeated. If
Creed lost against the foe that stalked him, then she
would also lose, for he would leave her.

But it was too late to weigh and measure, view pro
and con, right and wrong. The directives from her
mind were intermingled with those from her heart, and
her heart spoke with the louder voice.

"I can't tell you to stay away from me, Creed," she
whispered. "I just can't."

With a moan, he gathered her into his arms and
brought his lips to hers. Her hands splayed over his
back, feeling the corded muscles beneath the T-shirt,
as their tongues met in the sweet darkness of her
mouth. It was as though he were stealing the breath
from her body, and replacing it with the heat emanating from his rugged frame. It created a liquid fire
of need, of desire, that rambled throughout her.

"You'd better," Creed said, taking a ragged breath,
"go tend to your babies."

"My who?" she said, her voice unsteady. "Oh, yes, my darling dolls. I've got to finish the order for —"

"Shh," Creed said, as his head snapped around to stare at the front door.

He moved swiftly to the window, staying out of view as he brushed back the curtain. Had they come after him already? he thought, his jaw tightly clenched. Damn it, had they found him so soon? He'd covered his tracks, made it appear he was headed for Greece, then circled back.

"It's one of the harvest crew trucks," he said under his breath, then silently cursed. He'd done it again. He'd reacted on instinct, and Dawn had witnessed it. He was going to turn around and see the fear in her eyes, the questions, the doubts. She deserved explanations. She had the right to know who it was who kept pulling her into his arms, kissing her, stirring her hidden desires. But how could he explain what made no sense to himself? What could he say that would make it all disappear, bring a smile back to her lips, the warmth to her dark eyes? Nothing.

Creed turned slowly, postponing the moment when he would see in Dawn's eyes, on her face, what he knew would be there.

"Well," she said, a little too loudly, "I'm off. I'll never get that order completed on time if I don't get to work. The banister looks great, Creed. Max will be pleased with it, and the front steps, too."

"Dawn, I—"

"No, don't," she said, shaking her head. "Let me pretend I didn't see that. I said I'd give you time, and I will, but the questions are screaming at me, and I don't know where to put them. So much is happening so quickly, that I'm probably having a nervous breakdown, and I don't even know it. I really need to go home, be alone for awhile.''

"I understand."

"Creed," she said, her voice trembling, "did you bring it with you? The gun? Is it here in this house?''

"Yes," he said quietly, "it's here."

"Good."

"What?" he said, obviously confused.

"Whoever you thought was outside that window, I don't want them to hurt you. I really couldn't handle it if they hurt you," she said, blinking back sudden tears.

"Oh, Dawn, they..."

"I've got to go," she said, turning and running from the room.

"Ah, man," he said, "what am I doing to her?"

Halfway through the woods on the way to the Gilbert farm, Dawn sank to the ground and leaned her back against a tree. Her legs were trembling so badly they refused to hold her, and her heart raced beneath her breast. She felt as though she were caught in quicksand, unable to free herself. Her breath came in short gasps, and she pressed her fingertips to her throbbing temples.

The situation was worse, far worse, than Creed just running from himself. He was also fleeing from people who wished him harm. When she'd asked him if he had his gun, she had thought only of his safety. She hadn't cared if he'd done something wrong, if those pursuing him had every legal right to do so. She hadn't cared! She couldn't bear it if something happened to him! Oh, dear heaven, was she really in love with

Creed? Was it love causing these tempestuous emotions within her? How was she to know?

"Oh, God," she said, sinking her face into her hands, "I can't deal with all of this." Why had he come back? Why couldn't Creed have just stayed wherever he'd been, written his letters to Max, let them all go on with their lives as they were? He had no right to... But yes, he did. This was his home, Max was his father. Creed could not be held responsible for her reactions to him, the instant attraction, the pull on her senses, the heightening of her passion. She had gone into his embrace willingly. He had given her the opportunity to walk away from him, and she'd refused.

She would grant him the time and trust she'd promised to him.

Four

At midnight, Dawn gave up her futile attempt to sleep, and walked to the open window of her second-floor bedroom, her gaze lingering on the star-studded sky. The sound of a cricket's serenade filled the night, and an owl hooted in the distance. The smells of the farm intertwined, hanging heavy in the hot, humid air.

The Gilberts' home was almost identical to the Parkers' in size, the farms themselves both 125 acres. The friends grew the same crops, had fifteen dairy cows each, kept chickens and raised hogs for market. But now there was a sudden and disturbing difference between the two stretches of land. The Parker farm had Creed.

Dawn sighed as she lifted her hair from her neck, hoping for a cooling breeze. The image of Creed danced before her eyes, and she knew that no firm mental directive would chase it away. Through the

no sense of purpose, direction. I followed Orv around
the farm, but I was as useful as an extra foot. The first
time Elaine sent me out to gather eggs, I ended up
flying out of that chicken coop screaming my head off
because a chicken came after me. Oh, my,'' she said,
laughing softly, ''I was a dud.''

''And?'' Creed said, chuckling. ''Elaine sent you
right back in and said to show that chicken who was
boss.''

''Exactly. The chickens are my full responsibility
now. And, I will have you know, I was the one who
got the best price for Orv and Max's hogs last year.''

''Good for you.''

''Anyway, I still had a lot of time on my hands. My
fancy schooling was useless on the farm. One day,
Elaine asked if I'd help her with making some new
kitchen curtains. Me, who had never sewn a stitch.
Turned out I had a natural flair for it. We were going
to Tuckers' farm for a cookout for their little girl's
birthday, and I started playing around with fabric
scraps Elaine had in a box. I made a cute little doll all
decked out in a party dress. Amy Tucker adored it,
and I had such fun making it.''

''And you were on your way.''

''Yes. I experimented with differed styles, then decided that no two of my dolls would be the same. Each
would be unique. Word spread, and Amy's friends all
wanted one. Then I got terribly brave and took some
into Madison to a boutique. They accepted a half
dozen on consignment, and they sold in a week.''

''Whew!''

''Now I have orders from three stores and several
others have approached me, but I have all the business I can handle. I've turned one of the bedrooms

afternoon hours while she worked on the dolls, the thought of Creed had hovered in her mind. Through dinner, then the evening, he had been there. When she crawled between the cool sheets of her bed, he had stayed close, so close that her breasts grew taut beneath her nightie at the remembrance of his kiss and touch.

Creed Maxwell Parker was home. And Dawn Gilbert knew beyond a shadow of a doubt that she would never be the same again.

Her gaze shifted to the woods that separated the two farms. "Good night, Creed," she said. "Sleep well, my love." With a shuddering breath, she wrapped her hands around her elbows, as tears blurred her vision.

She was in love with Creed Parker.

In the quiet of the summer night, there was no escape from what she knew to be true. She loved him. She loved a man of secrets, of lies. A man with icy blue eyes that spoke of a pain that was ripping him to shreds.

But those eyes were warm pools of blue when he smiled at *her*, smoky with desire when he wanted *her*. *She* brought him from the shadows of his demons, and made him laugh. He considered himself a man alone, but he wasn't, because she loved him. Together they could face the demons of his past, beat them, be named the victors, then look to their future. Together.

Creed cared for her, she knew he did. That message was clear each time he took her in his arms. He might even be in love with her, but he was ignoring the whispers of his heart. Oh, yes, she would give him time and trust, but with them would be the strongest power known to humankind: love. She didn't care who Creed was or what he'd done. It didn't matter, because he was home now, safe. And she loved him.

A gentle smile formed on Dawn's lips as she moved back to the bed and slipped between the sheets. Creed's image seemed real enough to touch, and with that thought, she slept.

In the rosy glow of first light, Dawn made her way through the woods to the swimming hole. In spite of her few hours' sleep, she felt alive and carefree, bursting with energy. Her senses seemed strangely alert, magnifying the sights, sounds, smells around her. Her skin tingled, her eyes were sparkling. She was in love, and it was glorious. Her laughter danced through the air, clear, uninhibited, the resonance of one whose joy came from within.

At the edge of the water, she dropped her robe to the ground, relishing the warmth of the rising sun as it caressed her naked body. She pulled the ribbon from her hair, then moved into the pond.

His gift from the dawn, Creed thought, as he watched from the trees.

He'd slept restlessly, tossing and turning through the hours of the seemingly endless night. He had not been beleaguered by images from the past, but instead had seen only Dawn, heard her laughter, felt the heat of desire course through him as he remembered the feel and taste of her mouth on his. Awake and unable to tolerate the confines of his room, he'd tugged on jeans and a T-shirt and left the house, walking through the woods in the eerie first light. Standing by the swimming hole, he replayed over and over in his mind the moment he had seen Dawn Gilbert. A splash of color

caught his eyes, and he reached into the grass to re-
trieve the blue ribbon she had taken from her hair. He
smiled, then placed the ribbon in his pocket.

At the sound of Dawn's approach, Creed had
moved to the cover of the trees to watch her in the
morning ritual. It felt right, good, that he stood guard
over her while she swam naked. He belonged there,
protecting her, because she was his lady, he was her
man.

In the serene setting of the quiet woods at day-
break, Creed Parker knew he was in love with Dawn
Gilbert. He took the knowledge unto himself slowly,
sifting it through his mind, his heart, then his soul,
savoring the warmth it brought to each section of his
being. Savoring the peace. No ghosts were allowed
entry as he drank in the sight of the vision of loveliness before him, the only woman he had ever loved.

Creed moved out of the trees and walked to the edge
of the pond. Dawn was floating on her back, her eyes
closed and a smile on her lips. He spoke reverently, a
husky timbre to his voice, as he said aloud the name
of the one who had captured his heart forever.

"Dawn."

The hushed sound of his voice enfolded Dawn almost like a cloak of velvet caressing her, comforting
and exciting her in the same breathless moment. Creed
was there. If she opened her eyes she would see him
standing before her so strong, so ruggedly handsome,
so magnificent in his male splendor.

Dawn slowly lowered her feet as she lifted her lashes
to reveal her brown eyes that glistened with sudden
tears. A soft smile formed on her lips as Creed extended his hand toward her, his icy blue eyes trans-

formed into warm, tender, welcoming pools the color
of the sea.

She walked toward him, their gaze meeting as she
rose from the cool water, the moisture clinging like
dewdrops to her satin skin. The wet cascade of her hair
tumbled to her waist and fell across the full mounds of
her bare breasts, as she placed her hand in Creed's and
stood before him.

For a seemingly endless moment they simply stood
there, hardly breathing, as pulses skittered and heartbeats quickened. Then Creed cradled her face in his
large hands, brushing his lips over hers, then kissing
her cheeks, forehead, before moving to the slender
column of her throat. She gasped in pleasure as he
filled his hands with her breasts, then lowered his
mouth to draw first one then the other rosy bud into
the darkness. Tilting her head back, Dawn closed her
eyes to savor the sweet torture of his tongue and teeth
working their magic on the soft flesh. The seductive
rhythm was matched by the pulsing beat deep in the
core of her femininity.

She gripped his powerful shoulders for support, as
a moan escaped from her lips. Creed lowered her
slowly to the plush grass, stipping off his clothes before stretching out next to her.

"Beautiful," she said, her voice whisper soft. Her
gaze swept over his magnificent, bronzed body. His
manhood was a bold announcement of his need, his
want of her. And she loved him. "You are so beautiful, my Creed," she said.

"You are the beautiful one," he said, his voice gritty
with passion. "You are my gift from the dawn. Now
you are giving me yourself, Dawn's gift. Your name is

so right. Dawn is a beginning, a newness, a fresh start. That's what you are to me.''

"Oh, Creed," she said, lifting her arms to his.

In a languorous journey, he kissed and caressed every part of her lissome body. His lips trailed a heated path over her skin, that was matched by the liquid fire of need within her. She, too, explored the exquisite mysteries of Creed's taut, muscular body, marveling at his perfection, anticipating the sensual promise of what would be hers. As his hand slid to the inner warmth of her thighs, she moved restlessly, her breathing erratic, cheeks flushed.

"Creed, please!"

"Yes!"

His mouth sought her breasts once more, then moved to her lips in a searing kiss. Then with a smooth thrust of power he entered her, filling her with his maleness, as she arched her back to bring him closer. The raging rhythm of their bodies thundered in a synchronized tempo—harder, stronger, building a tension of ecstasy.

"Creed!"

"Don't be afraid. I'm here. Hold on to me."

Dawn called to Creed again as the spasms rocketed throughout her in rippling waves. She dug her fingers into his corded arms to keep from floating into oblivion. An instant later, he shuddered above her, chanting her name, then collapsing against her, his energy spent. He pushed himself up on trembling arms to gaze at Dawn's face.

"Oh, Creed," she said, placing her hands on his cheeks. "I have never experienced anything like that. It was wonderful."

"*You* were wonderful," he said, kissing her tenderly.

He moved away, then tucked her close to his side, sifting his fingers through the damp, silken threads of her hair. Oh, how he loved her, wanted to cherish and protect her for the rest of his life. But to declare his love was to speak of a promise, a commitment, a future that they could share. And offer Dawn what? His ghosts, his emptiness, his search for himself?

Only when he was with her, was he complete. When he stood alone, he was a shell, held captive in his dark tunnel of confusion. To use Dawn as his only link to life, to inner peace, was wrong. He would continually take from her, drain her, give her nothing in return. Until he was whole, he had no right to speak of his love for the delicate creature he held in his arms. Their lovemaking had been like none before, a joining not only in body, but to Creed, in heart and soul as well. He must beat the foe, and the foe was himself.

"I'd like to stay right here all day," Dawn said, bringing Creed from his reverie.

"So would I. We've created a world of our own. Dawn, there's so much I want to say to you, but I can't find the words. Just know, believe, that what we shared was more important to me than I could ever begin to tell you."

"I understand, because I feel the same way. Creed, I know you have things you have to settle within yourself. But as you're sorting it all through, I think it's only fair that you know that I love you."

"Oh, Dawn," he said, tightening his hold on her.

"I'm not asking anything of you, Creed. My love for you is, well, mine. I don't care what you've done

in the past, because I love you for who you are now—
for who you are in regard to myself.''

"But, Dawn, I . . .''

"I will be here if you want to talk about whatever it
is that is causing your pain, but I won't push you for
answers if you choose not to give them. You are loved,
Creed Maxwell Parker. You are so very, very loved.''

With a throaty groan, Creed brought his mouth
sweeping onto Dawn's. The ember of desire burst instantly into a raging flame of passion that carried them
above reality, as they once again became one. Sated at
last, they lay close.

"We'd better make an appearance or our families
are going to send the Marines looking for us," Creed
said finally.

"I don't want to move.''

"Up, my lady," he said, reaching for his clothes.

"Are you coming over to our place? The harvest
crew is probably there by now.''

"No, I told Max I'd plow the fields. It's been many
years since I've driven a tractor. I hope I don't run into
a tree.''

"There are some things you never forget how to
do," Dawn said, stretching leisurely.

Creed chuckled, then got to his feet to dress. Dawn
pulled on her robe, then rose to stand in front of him,
where she was the recipient of a long, sensuous kiss
that left her trembling.

"See you soon," Creed said, close to her lips.

"Yes," she said, drawing a steadying breath.

Creed watched until she disappeared among the
trees, then he turned and walked slowly away in the
opposite direction.

Dawn's fervent hope that Elaine would be somewhere other than the kitchen was not fulfilled. The older woman looked up from where she sat working at the table the minute Dawn entered through the back door.

"I was getting concerned about you," Elaine said. "You usually aren't gone this long when you sneak off to Parkers' swimming hole."

"I lost track of time. I'll get dressed and be right back to help you make food for the crew. Won't take me a minute. I just need to rinse out my hair and—"

"Dawn, what's wrong? You're babbling."

"Wrong? Why, nothing. Nothing at all. Everything is fine. You do worry so," she said, kissing her aunt on the cheek.

"Do I? Max is here. He said Creed was nowhere in sight this morning."

"Oh?"

"My dear child, I don't want to see you get hurt. I realize that you and Creed are attracted to each other, but tread slowly, be sure you're listening to your mind as well as your heart. I came right out and asked Max if he thought Creed was troubled about something. Max said yes, but he won't approach Creed about it. Oh, Dawn, Creed won't even say how long he's staying. Don't you see? He could pack up and be gone tomorrow."

"No!" Dawn said, shaking her head. "He won't. He wouldn't just disappear. Not now."

"Oh, Dawn," Elaine said, sighing, "I knew it the minute you walked in that door. You made love with Creed."

he'd gone for his gun, and when he'd peered out the window at the sound of a vehicle? Who, what, stalked him? Would he ever be free to love her? Would he?

"Stop thinking!" she said, marching down the hall to the shower. "Just love Creed Maxwell Parker, and stop thinking!"

While Dawn and Elaine prepared the food for the harvest crew, an uncomfortable silence fell between them. For the life of her, Dawn could not come up with one thing to say in the form of idle chitchat that would draw her aunt's thoughts from the subject of Dawn and Creed. She knew Elaine was concerned about the outcome of Dawn's love for Creed, and Dawn was distressed to realize she was causing the dear woman such upset. But it took only a whisper of a thought of Creed Parker for Dawn to feel the warm glow once again within her.

At noon the food was carried to the crew, then Dawn packed a lunch for Creed in the wicker basket and set out through the woods for the Parker farm. The chugging sound of the tractor reached her as she crossed the rear lawn, and billows of dust marked the place in the field where Creed was plowing. She walked to the edge of the freshly turned earth, and waved her arm in the air as Creed swung the tractor back in her direction. He acknowledged her presence with a fist punched straight upward. Dawn laughed in delight.

His lovely, lovely Dawn, Creed thought, willing the lumbering machine to go faster. Their lovemaking had been incredible. What they had shared could not be put in mere words. The physical had been intertwined with the emotional, and he'd never experienced anything like it before. Ah, man, she was something, his Dawn. He loved her.

At the edge of the field, Creed shut off the tractor and swung to the ground in a smooth motion. He grabbed his shirt from the back of the seat and strode toward Dawn.

"Hello," he said, brushing his lips over hers. "I'll do a proper job of kissing you after I hose off this sweat and dirt. What's in the basket?"

"Lunch," she said. Creed was glistening with perspiration, creating rivers of moisture through the layer of dust on his broad, bare chest. He was, she decided, beautiful. "Are you hungry?"

Creed chuckled low in his throat. "What's on the menu?" he asked, wiggling his eyebrows at her.

"This and that," she said, batting her eyelashes, "and that and this."

"Sold!"

By the tree where Dawn had created her tub of lemonade, Creed turned on the hose and drenched his torso and head. As Dawn watched the intriguing play of muscles in his arms and back, a tingling sensation swept along her spine, and she swallowed heavily as desire rambled unchecked within her.

Oh, goodness, how she loved this man!

Creed turned off the water, then reached out his arm and circled Dawn's waist, pulling her up against him.

"You're all wet!" she said, flattening her hands on his chest.

"But I want my first taste of lunch," he said, then claimed her mouth with his.

The kiss was long and sensuous, and Dawn was trembling when Creed released her. Her cotton blouse was damp from being crushed to his chest, her breasts clearly outlined beneath the thin material. Creed's eyes swept over her, and the buds of her breasts grew taut, aching for his tantalizing touch.

"Ah, man," he said, "what you do to me."

"What you do to me," she said, taking a steadying breath.

"Food! Give me food before I ravish your body right here under this tree."

"Can we vote?" she said, smiling up at him.

He laughed, then slipped on his light blue shirt, leaving it unbuttoned and hanging free as he pulled her down next to him on a dry patch of grass. As he ate a thick sandwich and drank lemonade from a jar, Dawn watched his smile disappear, then change into a deep frown that knitted his dark brows together. Minutes passed, and Dawn began to chew nervously on her bottom lip.

"A Ping-Pong ball," Creed finally said, causing her to jump.

"Pardon me?"

"You said I was like a Ping-Pong ball, because I went back and forth. That's what's happening in my mind now. I keep having this tug of war with myself. A part of me feels it's very unfair to you to be involved with a man who is keeping secrets from you. Another section says that my problems are mine, I created them, I have to solve them. To dump them on you, tell you everything, is not right, either. Damn. I don't know what to do, Dawn, I really don't."

"Creed, I ..."

"I guess I have to face the fact that I have a fear of losing you after having just found you. You said that you love me as the man I am in regard to yourself. The only Creed Parker you know is the one who's here on this farm, with you, kissing, holding, making love to you. What about the other Creed? If you came to hate that side of me Dawn, what would become of your love?"

"Hate you? Creed, I love you! My love isn't conditional, only encompassing the good times. There is nothing you can tell me that is going to change how I feel about you."

"You don't know that!"

"Yes, I do!"

"Damn," he said, raking his fingers through his damp hair. "I'd be taking from you again, asking you to be a part of my dark tunnel. I thought, hoped, that by coming home I could settle things within myself, figure out where I got lost, know who I really am. If only I could explain it all to you in a neat package with everything straightened around in my head. But the void is there, that emptiness. I'm filling it with you, and not coming to terms with the ghosts like I'm supposed to. That's wrong, don't you see? I don't deserve your love, Dawn, not in the shape I'm in now."

"Then talk to me, Creed. We'll battle this thing together. It's all bottled up inside of you, and it's ripping you apart. What better person to share it with than the woman who loves you?"

"I should be protecting you, cherishing you, not dragging you through this garbage. Your love is a gift and I don't want to lose it."

"Which is better? For me to know the truth, or guess about what is bothering you? I'm human, Creed. There's times when it sneaks up on me, frightens me. I've seen your razor-sharp reflexes, and I've seen you automatically reach for a gun. I also know there's someone, or a lot of someone's, after you. I push it all away, concentrate on you, us, then I see the pain in your eyes and it rushes back on me. Ghosts take up too much room. They're there, hovering around, seeming to get bigger, stronger. Oh, Creed, please! Tell me everything. Tell me!''

The play of emotions that crossed Creed's face spoke of his inner struggle, his desperate effort to sort through the jumble in his mind. Dawn stared at him intently, sending mental messages to him to take her into his arms and talk to her, bare his soul, allow her to help him.

Please! her mind begged. *Please, Creed!*

He rolled to his feet in a smooth, powerful motion, then shoved his hands into his pockets, his back to Dawn. His shoulders were set in a tight, hard line, his neck a thick column as he held himself rigid. The tension emanating from his rugged body seemed to work its way into Dawn's, causing her to shiver as she watched him. Seconds, then minutes ticked by, and an ominous silence fell. Hardly breathing, her heart thundering beneath her breast, Dawn waited, her gaze riveted on the tall man before her.

Creed drew a deep, shuddering breath. "No," he said, "I can't do it. It would be like describing a bad movie to you, then announcing I don't know how it ended. Better for you to have none of the facts, than just some. The piece of the puzzle that's missing, is me. This isn't going to work, my being here."

"What are you saying?" she whispered, a knot tightening in her stomach.

"I'm using you, Dawn. I'm using you and your love to bring me inner peace. I'm still running from myself. I've got to leave, go somewhere else, so I'll have to face this thing head on."

"No!" she said, scrambling to her feet as quick tears filled her eyes.

"Yes," he said, turning and gripping her by the shoulders. "It's the only way. We have no future together until I'm a whole man again."

"Don't leave!" she cried, tears spilling over onto her cheeks. "Oh, please, don't do this."

"I have to! We can't survive this way. I'll work it out somehow, then tell you everything. You'll have a choice then, Dawn, as to whether you still want me. I can't ask you to stay with me until I have something to offer you. If I find Creed Maxwell Parker, I'll come back and explain it all to you."

"And if you don't find yourself, your peace? What then?" she said, choking on a sob.

"I'll contact you, let you know, but I won't step back into your world again, Dawn."

"No, no, no!" she said, wrapping her arms around his waist and burying her face in his chest.

He circled her shoulders with his arms and pressed his hand to the back of her head, holding her tightly.

"I'm so sorry," he said, his voice strained. "I've made you cry. I've hurt you. The last thing I ever wanted to do was hurt you. I've taken so much from you, and given you nothing in return."

"That's not true. It's not! You've shown me what it means to be in love, truly happy. You're treating me like a child, who has to be shielded from anything unpleasant. I'm a woman, your woman, and I love you!"

And he loved her, Creed thought. He had to leave, because he loved her. Her tears were caused by him. He'd made her cry. He had no right to make Dawn cry. In his own way, he was abusing her, just like the scum she'd been married to.

"Listen to me," he said, tilting her head up and looking into her tear-filled eyes. "I've got to do this. I'm going to finish plowing the field, then go tell Max. You said you'd give me time and trust. You meant that, didn't you?"

"Yes, of course."

"Time and trust, Dawn," he said, lowering his lips to hers.

Dawn returned the kiss feverishly, wrapping her arms tightly around Creed's neck. An irrational part of her mind told her that while she held him, he couldn't leave her, while she kissed him, he couldn't go. She leaned against him, molding herself to him, clinging to the man she loved as tears streamed down her face.

Creed lifted his head, then cradled her face in his hands.

"Don't cry anymore," he said, his voice gritty with passion. "Please don't cry anymore. Those aren't cleansing tears, they're tears of pain, and I caused them."

Dawn took a deep, wobbly breath before she attempted to speak. "You're right," she said, "I'm falling apart here. I said I wasn't a child, but I'm acting like one. I'm supposed to be helping you, not adding further concern. You do whatever you must, and I'll wait. I will wait, Creed. Time and trust? Yes, you have them. And my love. Forever."

"Oh, Dawn."

"You'll leave tonight?"

"Yes. I think that will be easier on everyone."

"What about Max?"

"He probably knows something is wrong, but he won't ask for an explanation. My silence is kinder at this point."

"Will I see you before you go? Oh, damn it, Creed, I hate this! I hate everything about it! I want to stamp my foot and throw a tantrum, do something, anything, to keep you here."

"That's better," he said, smiling at her. "Get mad as hell, Dawn Gilbert."

"I am!"

"Good! You'll do okay angry, rather than sad. You can pop me in the chops if you want to."

"Don't tempt me," she said, then sniffled as she brushed the tears off her cheeks. "How can one man make me so happy and so miserable at the same time? My life would be so much simpler if you'd turned out to be a beautiful bum sleeping in the green room."

"What?"

"Nothing. I don't suppose you're going to tell me where you'll be?"

"No."

"Didn't think so," she said, sighing.

"I'll— Someone is coming through the woods," he said, his head snapping around.

"Don't you dare do your superman reflexes number, Creed Parker! I've had all I can take for one day."

"When you get mad, you don't mess around," he said, grinning at her.

"You'd better believe it."

Suddenly a figure emerged from the trees, running at full speed. Creed frowned and moved Dawn behind him, as the young man came barreling up to where they stood.

"Creed Parker?" he said, gasping for breath.

"Yeah."

"Mr. Gilbert sent me for you. I'm part of the harvest crew. It's your father, Max. He's collapsed. Mr. Gilbert thinks it's a heart attack."

"Damn it!" Creed said, then took off at a run toward the woods.

"Dear heaven, no!" Dawn said. "Not Max!"

In the next instant, Dawn started running in the direction Creed had taken. Her own anguish was forgotten, her thoughts now focused on dear, loving Maxwell Parker.

"I'm *in* love with Creed," she said, lifting her chin to a determined tilt. "That makes a tremendous difference, Aunt Elaine."

"And Creed? Does he love you?"

"He cares very deeply for me, I know he does. Creed and I are not children. We know what we're doing."

"No, you're not children. Their hurts can be soothed by a hug and a Band-Aid. The pains adults suffer are far greater. I don't want that to happen. Not to you, not to Creed. I love you both."

"We're fine, really we are. I've never been so happy. Creed is everything and more than I'd ever hoped to find in a man."

"Is he? Just how much do you actually know about him?"

"Enough to have fallen in love with him. I'll get dressed," Dawn said, hurrying from the room.

"Oh, Dawn," Elaine said quietly, "I do worry."

In her room, Dawn refused to replay in her mind the conversation with Elaine. Nothing, *nothing*, was going to destroy the memories of the lovemaking shared with Creed. Her body still hummed with the sensual joy of having been kissed, touched, filled by the man she loved. He had shown her the true meaning of the coming together of man and woman, a splendor like none she had ever experienced before. She had waited a lifetime for Creed, and now he was there.

But for how long? her inner voice asked. No! She wouldn't dwell on that, nor on what plagued Creed, brought the icy emptiness to his blue eyes. He had spoken of the dawn and of her, as beginnings, fresh starts. So be it. The past was just that . . . in the past. But was it? Whom had Creed been expecting when

Five

————

The University Hospital in Madison was a beehive of activity, but the four people waiting for news of Max Parker's condition were oblivious to the hubbub. In a designated area near the emergency room, Dawn, Creed, Elaine and Orv sat in numbed silence.

By the time Dawn had made her way through the woods to the Gilbert farm, Creed had placed an unconscious Max in the back seat of the Gilbert car. Orv sat next to his dear friend while Creed drove the forty miles into Madison. Dawn and Elaine followed in the pickup truck, neither speaking as Dawn drove above the speed limit.

And now they waited.

Dawn watched as Creed pushed himself to his feet and walked to the window, bracing his hands on the frame and staring out. His jaw was clenched so tightly she could almost feel the pressure. The tension emanating from his rigid body seemed to crackle through the air. She longed to go to him, wrap her arms around him, tell him his father was going to be fine. But there was nothing she could say to erase the horror of the moment. She herself was a breath away from bursting into tears at the thought of anything happening to Max.

Dawn pressed her fingertips to her temples, drew a deep, steadying breath and waited.

Why? Creed thought fiercely. Why Max? No, that wasn't fair. There weren't answers to questions like that, no blame to be placed. Unless... Had Max's concern for Creed's obviously troubled state of mind brought on this attack? Had he done this to his father with his selfish act of coming home like a frightened boy? Should he place Max's name next to Dawn's as people he had hurt by his arrival?

"Damn," he said, running his hand down his face. He shouldn't have come back. But if he'd stayed away, he wouldn't have discovered Dawn. No, he shouldn't have come back. But what if Max's heart attack had been inevitable, and Creed had been halfway around the world when his father needed him? Or had the attack been Creed's fault? Damn, the Ping-Pong ball was bouncing back and forth in his mind again. Back and forth. Pounding against his brain.

"Mr. Parker? Creed Parker?" a man said.

"Yes," Creed said, spinning around as the others got immediately to their feet.

"I'm Dr. North," the gray-haired man said, coming forward and extending his hand.

Creed shook the doctor's hand absently. "My father?" he said. "How is he?"

"I won't mince words. He's very ill. He's had a massive heart attack, and is in critical condition."

"Oh, God," Dawn whispered, clutching Elaine's hand.

"All we can do," the doctor continued, "is see what happens in the next twenty-four hours. We can't ignore the fact that this isn't Max's first heart attack, and there's already been damage done to—"

"Wait a minute," Creed said. "What do you mean, this isn't his first attack?"

"Max has been my patient for over a year. He came to me complaining of chest pains and fatigue. I ran tests, which indicated he'd had a mild heart attack. I wanted to hospitalize him, but he refused."

"Did you know about this, Orv?" Creed said.

"No, son. Max never said a word."

"I don't understand this!" Creed said. "Why would Max keep something so important from us?"

"Easy, Creed," Orv said. "Let the doctor finish."

"Well," Dr. North said, "there isn't that much to say. Max saw me once a month, and I began to detect a general weakening of his heart. There really wasn't anything I could do, except advise him to rest the moment he felt tired. In all honesty, this attack doesn't surprise me. I just wish it hadn't been so severe."

"Could stress, worry, have brought it on?" Creed said, a pulse beating in the strong column of his neck.

"Don't do it, Creed," Elaine said. "You're looking to blame yourself for this and you shouldn't. Max has been a happy man since you got home. You're not responsible for what happened."

"No one is," Dr. North said. "The heart's a muscle, and Max's is damaged, worn out. He knew he was running a risk by refusing to be hospitalized last year, but he said he was staying on his farm where he belonged. I had to respect him for that. He knew what he wanted to do, and he did it. That's all I can tell you. Now, it's wait and pray.''

"May I see him?" Creed said.

"Only through the window. If he holds on for the next twenty-four hours, I'll move him to the cardiac care unit, but for now he's in isolation, where someone will be with him every minute."

"Okay," Creed said, taking a deep breath. "Thank you."

"I'll keep you posted," Dr. North said.

"Yeah," Creed said, as the doctor left the room.

"Oh, Creed," Dawn said, blinking back her tears. "None of us knew that Max was ill."

"I know," Creed said, extending his hand to her. "Come here. You're white as a ghost."

"It's such a nightmare," she said, moving to his side. Creed circled her shoulders with his arm and held her tightly. "Max has got to be all right. He just has to, Creed. Oh, I'm sorry. I'm acting like a child again. I want to wave a magic wand and make all of this disappear. Well, I'm not going to fall apart. I just wish there was something I could do."

"You're doing it," Creed said quietly, "by loving him, caring so deeply."

"Creed," Orv said, "as much as I want to stay, I'd best get back to tend to the farms. There are chickens and hogs to feed, cows to be milked."

"I can't ask you to take all that on," Creed said. "That's double work."

"I'll help him," Elaine said. "We're better off busy than sitting here stewing. You call us if there's any change in Max's condition. If we're outside, keep phoning until you reach us. You can stay here with your father, and put your mind at ease about the chores. Dawn, are you coming with us?''

"No, I'm staying.''

"Dawn, no," Creed said. "There's no point in it. Go on home and get a good night's sleep.''

"I'm staying," she said firmly, looking up at him. "I want to be here.''

Creed studied her face for a moment, then nodded. "All right," he said. "I can see that your mind is made up.''

"We'd best be getting back to the farms," Orv said.

"Call us, Creed," Elaine added, squeezing his hand.

"I will, and thank you both.''

"We love Max," Elaine said. "It's as simple as that.''

Creed watched as Elaine and Orv left the room, then looked down at Dawn.

"I'm going to see Max through that window," he said. "I'll be back in a few minutes.''

Dawn nodded, then sank onto the sofa as Creed walked away. How quickly things can change, she thought ruefully. For reasons of his own, Max had kept the facts of his ill health to himself. Like Creed, Max had secrets, had chosen not to share what he knew. The Parker men were strong, independent and, yes, stubborn. She loved Max as she would a father. She loved Creed as a man, *her* man, the extension of herself. And at any given moment, she could lose them both.

"Don't you cry again, Dawn Gilbert," she said aloud. "Creed has enough problems without you blubbering. Knock it off.''

Creed stared through the isolation-room window, his eyes flickering over the elaborate equipment surrounding his father's bed. Max looked so small and old, he mused. He'd seemed to weigh nothing at all when Creed had lifted him into his arms to carry him to the car. Why hadn't Max told him about the heart attack of the year before? Didn't a son have the right to know that his father was ill? No, not really. Max was a man, not just a father. A man with decisions to make as he saw fit, just as Creed had done. And Maxwell Parker was a helluva of a man.

"Be tough, Dad," Creed said softly. "Fight like hell."

Creed walked slowly back to the waiting room, then stopped in the doorway, looking at Dawn where she sat on the sofa. A handful of hours ago he'd told her he was leaving. And she'd cried. Now her tears were for Max. So much love radiated from her. She was so giving, trusting. Well, now he was staying, because Max needed him. His own inner struggles would go on hold, all energies directed toward his father.

"Creed?" Dawn said, glancing up and seeing him in the doorway. "How is he?"

"I don't know," he said, walking to the sofa and sitting down next to her. "The same, I guess. They've got him all wired up to machines. He's lying there so damn still, and he looks old, Dawn. Old and tired."

"I hope you're not blaming yourself for this. Your coming home was a joyous time for Max. His eyes have been sparkling ever since you came. I just wish he'd told us about the first heart attack."

"I can understand why he kept it to himself. For the first time, I'm stepping back and viewing Max as a man, not just my father. We're more alike than I ever realized.''

"Stubborn."

"True," he said, smiling at her, "but loveable. Right?"

"Oh, yes," she said, leaning her head on his shoulder, "very, very loveable."

Creed picked up her hand and laced his fingers through hers. "I'm sure it goes without saying that I'm not leaving tonight. I guess I'll never really know if my coming back in the shape I'm in moved the timetable up on Max, but at least I'm here now, when he needs me. When my mother died, I left him high and dry. I haven't been the greatest son in the world."

"Max is very proud of you, Creed."

"No," he said, his voice hushed, "Max is proud of who he thinks I am, who I present myself to be. His son, the foreign diplomat, deserves Max's praise, and that person doesn't exist."

"Oh, Creed," Dawn said, sighing.

"Enough of that. It's dinner hour and we'd better get some food. Dawn, I really think you should go back to the farm. It's going to be a long night."

"No."

"Don't accuse a Parker of being stubborn, Gilbert," he said, getting to his feet and pulling her up beside him. "You win first prize in that category."

"Have I been insulted?"

"No," he said, brushing his lips over hers, "you've been kissed."

"I was? I missed it."

"Pay attention this time," he said, lowering his mouth to hers.

TAKE 4 FREE BOOKS
WHEN YOU PEEL OFF THE BOUQUET
AND SEND IT ON THE POSTPAID CARD

Elaine Camp's HOOK, LINE AND SINKER. Roxie was a reporter for *Sportspeople*. Sonny was the country's top fisherman and the subject of Roxie's latest interview. It wasn't long after they met that Roxie promised herself that Sonny would not become the one that got away.

Diana Palmer's LOVE BY PROXY. When Amelia walked into Worth Carson's boardroom wearing just a belly dancer's outfit, Worth fired her. What Amelia didn't know was that the handsome business tycoon was determined to have her — but only on his own terms.

Joan Hohl's A MUCH NEEDED HOLIDAY. For Kate Warren, Christmas was a lonely time — until she met handsome Trace Sinclair. And what had been a contest of wills began to change into something else, something only their hungry hearts dared admit . . . and would not let rest.

Laurel Evans' MOONLIGHT SERENADE. Emma enjoyed life in the slow lane, running a radio station in a small town. So, when TV producer Simon Eliot asked her to give a speech in New York, she refused. Why did Simon return every weekend? And why did Emma look forward so to his visits?

OPEN YOUR DOOR to these exciting, love-filled, full-length novels. They are yours *absolutely FREE along with your Folding Umbrella and Mystery Gift.*

AT-HOME DELIVERY. After you receive your 4 FREE books, we'll send you 6 more Silhouette Desire novels each and every month to examine FREE for fifteen days. If you decide to keep them, pay just $11.70 (a $13.50 value) — with no additional charge for home delivery. If not completely satisfied, just drop us a note and we'll cancel your subscription, no questions asked. **EXTRA BONUS:** You'll also receive the Silhouette Books Newsletter FREE with every book shipment. Every issue is filled with interviews, news about upcoming books, recipes from your favorite authors, and more.

Take this beautiful
FOLDING
UMBRELLA
with your 4 FREE BOOKS
PLUS A MYSTERY GIFT

The kiss was long and sensuous, leaving them breathless. Creed drew in a deep breath, let it out slowly, then went to inform the nurse on duty that he would be in the cafeteria if they needed him. The meal consisted of tasteless food and little conversation, their thoughts never straying far from Max.

Later, Dawn swallowed her tears as she stood by Creed's side and looked at Max through the window. Dr. North appeared, informed them there was no change in Max's condition, then Creed called Orv to convey the message.

The long night began.

An almost eerie hush fell over the hospital as the lights were dimmed slightly and the visitors disappeared. New faces appeared at the nurses' station as the shift changed. The emotionally draining day played its toll on Dawn, and at midnight she curled up in the corner of the sofa and dozed.

A restless energy surged through Creed and he paced the floor, finally stopping to stare out the window at the lights of the city. As he jammed his hands into his pockets, his fingers closed over the blue ribbon he had found in the grass by the swimming hole. He pulled it free, then gazed at it in the palm of his hand.

Exquisite pictures of Dawn and their lovemaking replayed in his mind as he ran his fingertips over the satin material. What was to become of them? His plan to leave had been a difficult choice, but the right one, and now it was impossible for him to go. The course of his life had come to an abrupt halt, then headed in a different direction when Max had been struck down.

The danger lay, Creed realized, in his knowing that he could find peace within himself when he was with

Dawn. A peace not earned, fought for and won, but given to him as yet another of Dawn's gifts. And it was wrong. He would once again be living a lie, presenting himself as someone he was not. He must resist the urge to seek solace in her love. To be worthy of Dawn's love, he had to be complete, a total entity unto himself, so he could give as well as take. Only then could he tell her that he loved her, wanted to be with her always as her husband, father of children they would create together. Only then. And it might never come to be.

Creed shook his head and frowned, then placed the ribbon carefully in his pocket. He walked to the sofa and stood watching Dawn sleep, a gentle smile tugging at his lips. Once again he saw the enchanting combination of child and woman, sensuous woman. With her hair in those thick braids, she appeared far younger than her twenty-six years, but the lush curves of her body, the full breasts pushing against the cotton blouse, gave testimony to her maturity.

Creed was filled with a coiling need, not just one of physical desire, but more. He desperately wanted to regain control of his life, right the wrongs, set everything in order. As it was, nothing was in its proper place, no section of his existence functioning as it should. His father lay close to death. His lady, his love, was unobtainable to him. He himself was an emotional wreck. A frustration, a cold fury, were building within him, bringing beads of sweat to his brow. He wanted to rage against the injustices, use his strength to beat them into submission, restore peace where there was chaos.

"Mr. Parker?" a nurse said from the doorway, bringing Creed from his thoughts.

"Yes. Has my father's condition changed?"

"No, no, your father is the same. I thought you might like these blankets and pillows."

"That's very kind of you," he said, taking them from her.

"You really should try to get some sleep. I'll wake you if there's any news. You're not going to do him any good by jeopardizing your own health."

"You're right. Thank you."

Creed tucked a pillow beneath Dawn's head, kissed her on the cheek, then placed a blanket over her. She stirred, then settled back into a deep sleep. He slouched into a leather chair and stretched his long legs out in front of him, crossing them at the ankles.

What the nurse said made sense, he supposed. There was no telling what tomorrow held, what there would be to face. Yeah, he'd better get some sleep.

He leaned his head back, closed his eyes and drifted off into a light, restless slumber.

The sound of voices woke Dawn and Creed at the same time, and they both sat up, not knowing where they were. Dawn groaned. Creed stood and stretched his neck back and forth, mumbling a few well-chosen expletives.

"Max," Dawn said, coming out of her foggy state.

"I'll go check on him right now," Creed said.

"Well, well," Dr. North said, coming into the room, "you two look worse than Max does this morning. Doesn't say much for this swanky hotel you stayed in."

"How is he?" Creed said.

"He had a good night, woke up for a minute or two and is resting comfortably. I'm pleased. His condition is stable at this point. I'm going to have him moved to cardiac care this morning. There's no reason to wait any longer. Max isn't out of the woods yet, Creed, but so far, so good.''

"Thank God," Dawn said.

"When can I see him? And I don't mean through a window," Creed said.

"The immediate crisis is over," the doctor said. "Now we'll monitor him very closely, and also get a true picture of how much damage was done to his heart. You can sit with him later today, if you like. I'd suggest you go home, then come back. You look like you spent the night here, and that might upset Max."

"Oh, okay," Creed said, running his hand over his beard roughened chin. "I guess I could pass as a . . ."

"Beautiful bum," Dawn said, smiling at him.

"I'll see you this afternoon," Dr. North said.

"Thanks, doc," Creed said.

"That's great news about Max," Dawn said, getting to her feet. "Isn't it?"

"Like the doc said, 'so far so good.' I guess these things are hard to predict, so they take it one step at a time. Come on. We'll go home and get some decent food. No sense eating the junk in this place if we don't have to."

"All right."

"By the way," he said, pulling her close, "you're nice to wake up to. You do realize that we just spent the night together."

"Relatively speaking," she said, smiling up at him. "I must look dreadful."

"You look lovely," he said, lowering his mouth to hers. In the next instant, he jerked his head up again. "Uh-oh," he said. "I forgot about my beard. I'm going to scratch you. Pretend I kissed you good-morning.''

"I don't have that vivid an imagination," she said, circling his neck with her arms. "I'd like to order one kiss, please, beard and all."

"Comin' right up," he murmured, then claimed her mouth. "Home. Now," he said, when he finally released her.

"'Kay," she said breathlessly, her heart racing.

Creed went to see Max once more through the window, while Dawn returned the blankets and pillows to the nurses' station. The fact that the curtain was drawn over the window brought Creed striding back down the hall with a deep frown on his face. He looked, Dawn decided, like an angry grizzly bear.

The morning air was remarkably cool, but the traffic was bumper to bumper as Madison's work force spilled onto the crowded streets. Creed maneuvered the old truck with skill, plus a patience that surprised Dawn. He continually waved drivers in ahead of him and voiced no objection at the snail's pace at which they were moving. The good ole farm boy in him, she mused, surfaced at the strangest times.

That thought caused Dawn to frown. So much had happened so quickly, that it had not yet occurred to her to look much further than the fact that she loved Creed. Her deepest hope and prayer was that he would calm his inner turmoil, then come to love her as she did him. And if that happened? What then? Years before, Creed had left the farm and its way of life to join the army. The traditional order of son stepping into his father's shoes to tend the land had not been followed. Creed had chosen a different road, one that had caused him pain, left him floundering.

And the future? What did he see for himself? Where
would he want to go? He was highly trained, Dawn
thought ruefully, for something that required split-
second reflexes and carrying a gun. Wonderful. Not
quite what was needed on the farm. Creed looked so
right, so natural, behind the wheel of a pickup, riding
a tractor, walking through the woods. That did not
indicate, however, that he wished to spend the rest of
his life on the Parker farm.

And Dawn? She'd had her fill of city life, society,
falderal, plastic smiles. Each time she went to Madison to shop or conduct business for Dawn's Dolls, she
registered a rush of relief when she returned to the
Gilberts'. The farm was her home, her haven, the place
where she could be herself, accepted as she was. She
loved the slower tempo it offered, the sights, sounds
and smells. There was meaning, purpose, in growing
the crops, an indescribable joy at witnessing the birth
of a calf or a litter of piglets. There were ongoing
promises of tomorrows as new life sprang forth. The
farm wasn't a place, it was a way of life. A way of life
Dawn never wished to leave.

"Oh, dear," she said, sighing.

"Problem?" Creed asked, glancing over at her.

"What? Oh, no, I was just thinking."

"There's a store a few miles up ahead that opens
early to cater to farmers. I need to stop and get something."

"Okay," she said. "Naturally you assume that my
female curiosity will get the better of me and I'll ask
what you suddenly need from the store."

"Yep."

"Forget it, chum."

Creed just chuckled.

Dawn lasted exactly three blocks.

"Darn it," she said, punching him in the arm, "why would a man who is probably half-starved and has spent the night in a chair, have an urge to go shopping?"

"Paint."

"Paint," she said, nodding. "Paint?"

"I'm going to paint the outside of the house. It looks pretty shabby, and it'll be a nice surprise for Max. No, don't say it, Dawn. I realize there are no guarantees that he'll live to see it, but it's something I want to do...either way."

"I understand," she said, smiling at him warmly, "and I think it's a lovely idea. In fact, I'll help you."

"Oh, yeah? Have you ever painted before?"

"No, but how tough can it be? Stick the brush in the paint, slap in on the house. Big deal."

"Oh, man," he said, laughing and shaking his head. "I'm headed for trouble here."

"We'll be a great team, you'll see."

"We *are* a great team," he said, his voice low. "What we have, what we've shared, in such a short period of time is more than some people have in years of being together. You're very important to me, Dawn. I want you to know that it meant a great deal to have you with me last night. I've been alone for so damn long, and I'm glad I've found you. I just wish... Well, one day at a time for now. There's the store." He loved this woman so much, he mentally tacked on. For the remainder of his life, he would love her.

Dawn's sigh was wistful. Such beautiful words, she mused, so full of promise, creating images in her mind of marriage, babies, endless years of happiness with Creed, working by his side to nurture their land and their love. Their love? No, he'd never said he loved her, there really were no promises, and the future was a foggy blur. All she had was each moment wherein she breathed with Creed. For now, it would have to be enough.

Inside the store, Creed headed for the section displaying paint, then with Dawn at his elbow he studied the color chart.

"What color do you think you want?" she asked.

"I don't know. Not white. It's always been white. Dingy, drab, dull, boring white."

"Goodness, I didn't think it looked *that* bad."

"Hey, wait a minute," he said, digging into his pocket and producing the satin ribbon. "Blue. A light, delicate shade of blue, just like this. What do you think?"

Dawn stared at the ribbon in Creed's hand. What did she think? That she'd shatter into a million pieces if this warm, tender, wonderful man left her. That he had depths that he himself was not fully aware of. That the same hand that knew a gun, found room for a pretty blue ribbon that had been hers. That she loved Creed Parker with every breath in her body.

"Hello?" Creed said.

"I think that blue would be very nice," she said, tears prickling at the back of her eyes.

"I'll go so far as to paint the trim white. Yeah, it'll be great. Max will love it."

"I'm sure he will," she said softly.

The supplies were purchased and loaded into the back of the truck. Creed found a pay telephone and called the hospital while Dawn waited in the truck. A sudden weariness swept over her, and she leaned her head back and closed her eyes.

Creed slid behind the wheel and turned the key in the ignition.

"They're moving Max to the cardiac care unit now," he said, driving out of the parking lot. "I told the nurse that if he woke up to tell him I'd be there this afternoon. She said that only immediate family can visit him."

"They won't let me see him?" Dawn said, lifting her head. "I'm like family, and so are Elaine and Orv. That's not fair! I love Max, and that must mean something to the people who make those stupid rules!"

"Hey, easy. You're getting all strung out. I'll talk to the doc about it, okay?"

"But what if they say no? Max has been like a father to me. I've seen him every day for the past three years while you were off God knows where and—" Dawn stopped speaking as she saw Creed's jaw tighten and his eyes narrow. "Oh, Creed, I'm sorry. I didn't mean that the way it sounded."

"I know I haven't been a terrific son for Max," he said tightly. "I don't need you to remind me of that fact."

"I said I was sorry! It just all caught up with me. I'm tired, and hungry and so worried about Max. I wasn't insinuating that you haven't been a good son."

"Weren't you?" he asked, his voice low.

"No! Max's world centers on you, and you know it. Every time he got a letter from you he'd bring it right over for all of us to see. And when you'd call he'd be smiling for days. He's proud of you."

"Of who he thinks I am!" Creed said, smacking his palm against the steering wheel. "The letters were full of lies, remember? You do remember that, don't you,

Dawn? Or have you conveniently forgotten, so it
makes it easier for you to be with me, allow me to kiss
you, touch you, make love to you?''

"Stop it!" she yelled. "You're the one consumed
with guilt over your lies, the life you led, whatever it
was. Why don't you test our love, Creed? Mine,
Max's, Elaine and Orv's. Why don't you tell the
truth?''

"Oh, good, great!" he said, with a snort of dis-
gust. "Just gather everyone around the kitchen table
and calmly announce that Creed Maxwell Parker,
whom you all know and love so very, very much, is a
killer!" *No!* his mind screamed. *Not like this! He
hadn't meant to tell her like this!*

Dawn felt as though she'd been struck by a crushing physical blow. The air seemed to swish from her
lungs, and a roaring noise echoed in her ears. Her entire body was heavy, as if it belonged to someone else
and wouldn't move under her command. She opened
her mouth, but no sound came out as she stared at
Creed.

Killer? her mind repeated. Creed killed people with
that gun he carried? That was ridiculous. What an as-
inine thing for him to say. He certainly had a strange
sense of humor at times. Creed wasn't a killer, for
heaven's sake. It was impossible. She loved him. "Oh,
dear God," she whispered, then a nearly hysterical sob
escaped from her lips.

"Dawn, please," he said, glancing over at her pale
face, then redirecting his attention to the traffic. "I'll
explain everything, all right? I had no intention of
dumping it on you like that. I'm so sorry! We'll be
home in a bit, then I'll start at the beginning. Dawn?''

"What?" she said, shaking her head slightly. "Were you saying something?"

Creed drew a shuddering breath. "No," he said, "nothing."

Dawn hardly remembered the remaining drive to the farm. A heavy silence hung in the truck, an oppressive silence, that made it difficult to breathe. She clutched her hands tightly in her lap and concentrated on taking air into her lungs, then letting it out, telling herself that if she failed to accomplish the ongoing task she would suffocate. Her head pounded with a steady cadence, adding further confusion to the jumble in her mind. Fragmented pictures danced before her eyes—scenes of Creed smiling, holding out his arms to her, then Creed gripping a gun, his features hidden by shadows, his expression unreadable. Bodies floated down in slow motion, bodies with no faces, no names, dead bodies. And Creed had killed them.

"Dawn, we're home," Creed said quietly, placing his hand on hers.

She stared down at the strong, tanned fingers, covering hers. They warmed her icy skin, and the heat traveled up her arms, creating a tingling sensation as it went, stroking her, waking her from her semi-trance.

"Creed?" she said, lifting her lashes to look at him.

"Yeah, babe, it's me. Let's get you inside, okay?"

"Oh, Creed," she said, flinging her arms around his neck as tears spilled onto her cheeks, "hold me. Please hold me. I'm so frightened. So frightened, Creed!"

He gathered her close to his chest, pressing his hand to the back of her head as she buried her face in his neck. He held her as if to never again let her go. She was there, in his arms, but he was alone. Incredibly

alone. The emptiness twisted like a knife in his gut, the
pain racking his mind and body. Every beat of his
heart thudded a single word in his brain. *Killer.*

He'd lived with the truth, suffered the agony of the
truth, but never before had he spoken it aloud, heard
his voice fill the air with the truth. The word itself was
lethal. He had seen the devastating effect it had had on
Dawn, the horror, the disbelief, and, oh, Lord, the
fear that had swept over her. And she was clinging to
him, trembling in his arms like a frightened child, a
broken bird, so fragile, vulnerable. What had he done
to her?

Creed's head snapped up as the front door of the
Gilbert house was pushed open and Elaine came out
onto the porch. He lifted his hand to motion her forward, and she hurried to the truck.

"Creed? Dawn?" she said, pulling open the door.
"What's wrong? Is it Max?"

"No, he's doing okay. He's stable, and had a good
night," Creed said, taking Dawn's arms gently from
his neck. "Dawn is just worn out, needs some food."

"Come on honey," Elaine said to Dawn. "Breakfast, a hot bath, then bed. Emotional fatigue is worse
than physical. Let me fix you a decent meal, Creed."

"No, thanks, I'll go on home. I'll bring the truck
back later after I unload the paint."

"Paint?" Elaine said.

"I'm going to paint the outside of the house for
Max. Blue. It's going to be a pretty blue. Elaine, take
care of Dawn. She's been through...a lot."

"Of course I will."

"I'll be going in to see Max this afternoon. The doc
isn't promising anything yet. I'll keep you posted."

"Creed?" Dawn said.

"Here now," Elaine said, "you come along with me, Dawn. Sure I can't feed you, Creed?"

"No, I'll get something at the house."

"We've been praying for Max," Elaine said.

"I know you have," he said, smiling slightly.

He crossed his arms over the steering wheel and watched as Dawn slid off the seat and walked into the house with Elaine's arm around her shoulders.

Don't go! his mind echoed over and over. Dawn, don't leave me, let me explain, let me tell you how it all happened. Dawn, please!

With a hand that was visibly shaking, Creed turned the key in the ignition and drove home, the silence of the house beating against him when he entered.

Dawn vaguely remembered eating, taking a warm bath, then allowing Elaine to slip a nightie over her head and tuck her into bed.

"I feel like a child," Dawn said.

"Doesn't hurt anyone to be fussed over a bit when they need it. You'll be good as new once you've had a nap."

"Will I?" she asked dully.

"Honey," Elaine said, sitting down on the edge of the bed, "I know you're worried about Max. We all are. We don't want him to be taken from us because we love him. But death is a part of life. If we lose him, we'll have to have faith, believe that it was meant to be."

"Death," Dawn said in a near-whisper. "There's all kinds of death, Aunt Elaine. Some are peaceful, gentle, coming at the end of full and happy lives. Other deaths are violent, horrible, deliberately brought about by a . . . a killer."

"Land's sake, what gruesome talk. Now you shut your mouth and your eyes, and get some sleep. I wish I had insisted that Creed eat. He looked terrible. You two put in a rough night. Well, food and rest, and you'll both be fine."

Nothing was fine, Dawn thought, as Elaine left the room. Nothing at all.

After shaving and showering, Creed pulled on clean jeans, remembering to take the blue ribbon from his pocket and place it on the dresser. He stared at it for a long moment before turning and striding from the room. He consumed several cups of coffee while finishing the remainder of the peach pie, then unloaded the paint from the back of the truck. And through it all, the Ping-Pong ball in his head went back and forth between thoughts of Dawn, then his father.

In the living room, he collapsed on the sofa and stared unseeing at a spot on the wall. Memories of his youth crept in around him: of his frail, gentle mother, of the laughter that had echoed within those walls. Oh, he'd been a handful, with his boundless energy and quick, mischievous mind. He'd given everything his maximum effort: schoolwork, chores, his love for his parents, the pranks he'd pulled. Life had been for living and he'd enjoyed it to the hilt.

Then the world beyond the farm had beckoned to him with its mysteries and undiscovered adventures. And so, he'd gone. With the blessings of the two most important people in his existence, he'd left the farm to take on the excitement of the unknown. As with everything else before, he'd plunged in at full steam. And then . . .

"Ah, hell," he said, getting to his feet, "not now. I've got to get some sleep."

Dawn's image followed him up the stairs, down the hall, settled next to him as he stretched out on the bed and laced his fingers under his head. He welcomed the desire that surged through him, the heat of it, the ache; it said he was alive, not just an empty shell masquerading in a man's body. He loved Dawn, wanted, needed her, and she could very well be lost to him forever.

The anger, frustration, began to build within Creed again, causing his heart to thunder, his pulse to race. He turned the rage inward on himself, for losing control of his life, for forgetting who he was. He moved the past years through his mind and frowned deeply at the chilling memories. As the knot in his gut tightened, he came to the present, to Dawn, to the brutal way in which he had flung the word "killer" at her with no regard for her feelings.

A strange, bitter sound erupted from his lips. How did one soften the title of "killer"? It was, *he was* everything it implied. Oh, sure, he'd told Dawn he would explain it all, how it had happened. Would she listen? What in the hell difference did it make? He didn't, couldn't, accept the truth about himself, so why should she? It was right that he should lose the love of Dawn Gilbert, because he'd never deserved to have it in the first place. He'd taken Dawn's gift of love and crushed it, destroyed it.

With a strangled moan, Creed rolled over onto his stomach. As if knowing he could bear no more, his mind went blank, giving way to sleep.

Six

_____

Elaine?" Creed said, entering the Gilbert kitchen.

"Oh, hello, Creed," she said, from where she was cooking at the stove. "You look much better."

"I slept for an hour. I brought the truck back. How's Dawn?"

"Quiet. She came down a few minutes ago and said she was going to work on her dolls. Are you leaving to go see Max now?"

"No. I called the hospital and they said they were running some tests on him, then he would have to rest. They asked me to wait a couple of hours before I came. Did Dawn say anything about this morning?" Creed asked, running his fingers through his hair.

"I figured there was more wrong with Dawn than just being upset about Max. Now, seeing you, I know there is. You frown any deeper your eyebrows are going to grow together. What happened between you and Dawn, Creed?''

"It's complicated, Elaine. I should never have come home, I guess. No, that's not true. Max needs me, and I'm glad I'm here. But Elaine, I never intended to hurt Dawn. I swear I didn't. She's the most wonderful woman I've ever met and I . . . I care a great deal for her."

"But?"

"Yeah, but," he said, leaning against the kitchen counter. "I'm not in a position to offer her a damn thing."

"Because of what's troubling you?"

Creed's head snapped up, then he straightened his stance and shoved his hands into his back pockets.

"Now, don't get in a snit," Elaine said. "Dawn didn't say a word to me. I knew the minute I saw you that something was wrong. You forget, Creed, I've known you since you were born. It's your eyes. They're different—cold, empty, hurting. You're a man carrying pain inside him, and those of us who love you can see that."

"Max, too? He definitely knows?"

"Of course he does. He's your father. He's waiting for you to come to him if you want to talk about it."

"Oh, no," Creed said, staring at the ceiling, "I've brought nothing but trouble."

"By bringing joy to Max by your being home? By making me and Orv mighty glad to see you? By bringing a glow of happiness like I've never seen before to our Dawn? That's what you've brought us, Creed."

"There are things you don't know."

"I realize that. But there's not been a problem made that couldn't be handled by love. Maybe not solved completely, but accepted, worked through. I think you're forgetting that."

"There's some things a man has to do alone."

"Maybe. Maybe not. Dawn's in her workroom upstairs."

"She probably prefers not to see me."

"You won't know unless you ask."

"You're a tough lady, Elaine," he said, smiling slightly.

"No, I love you like a son, and Dawn like a daughter. I want to see both of you happy."

Creed looked at the older woman for a long moment, then nodded and walked slowly from the room. Elaine pursed her lips together, wiped a tear from her cheek and continued cooking.

Upstairs, Creed went down the hall, glancing through the open bedroom doors. Then he saw her. Dawn was sitting in a rocking chair by the window, staring out over the farm. She was rocking slowly back and forth, a baby doll clutched to her breasts. Her hair was loose, a shimmering cascade of beauty tumbling to her waist, and she was wearing a long lightweight mint-green robe.

Creed stood in the doorway allowing the sight of Dawn to wash over him, cool his fury, ease his pain. The vision of loveliness before him was his love, his life. Had he lost her? Was it too late to reclaim what they'd had, then move tentatively forward? Was he destined to lose his lady and his father at the same time?

Creed moved into the room to stand by the rocker.

"Dawn?" he said quietly.

"Creed," she said, not looking at him, nor halting her back-and-forth motion in the chair.

"Would you rather I left you alone?"

"Who did you kill, Creed?" she said, turning her head to face him.

"It's a long story."

"Damn you!" she shrieked. "Who did you kill?"

"Men who were trying to kill me! That's how it's done, how the game is played. If you're quicker, smarter, luckier, you stay alive. If not, you're dead. The ones who took me on are dead!"

"Dear Lord," she whispered, "what kind of man are you?"

Creed backed away from her and took a deep breath. "I don't know," he said, his voice hushed. "I just don't know."

Dawn swallowed the lump in her throat as she saw the haunting pain settle on the icy pools of Creed's blue eyes. His voice was flat, weary sounding, and his shoulders slumped slightly as if their burden was too great to carry. Her fear and confusion were nudged aside, and replaced by love, tenderness, the want and need to comfort.

"Talk to me," she said. "Tell me everything. Make me understand."

"What I don't understand myself? How can I do that?"

"You're not alone anymore, Creed. I love you. It's unimportant whether or not I *should* love you, because it's too late to turn back. I'm asking you to tell me who you are, because I have a right to know. If you care for me at all, you'll tell me."

"Oh, Dawn," he said, "how can I say it in such a way that you won't hate me? I had such lofty ideals, such a sense of pride in what I was doing. I don't know where it all went wrong, when I changed, how I lost myself."

"Come sit by me," she said softly.

Creed gazed at her, their eyes meeting, holding. Before he realized he'd moved, he pulled the chair from near the sewing machine and placed it in front of her. He hesitated a moment, then swung his leg over the seat and sat down, propping his elbows on his knees and lacing his fingers loosely together. Staring at his long, tanned fingers, he began to talk.

"I was in intelligence in the army," he said quietly. "I was a natural for it, had some kind of uncanny sixth sense. After Vietnam I was approached by a man named Curry about joining a special, secret branch of our government. They'd been watching me carefully, and decided they wanted me. I became an agent, an operative, a highly trained . . . killer."

Dawn's hold on the doll tightened. "Go on," she said.

"I told my parents that I'd left the army for the diplomatic corps. And they believed me. My assignments for the first few years were lightweight stuff—making contact with deep-cover agents, quiet exchanges of smuggled documents—nothing fancy. Then, a deal went bad. I was set up by a double agent, who I met with in a back alley in France. He had two other men with him and they jumped me."

"Oh, Creed."

"I killed them," he said, his voice flat. "It was them or me, and I shot them. I couldn't believe it. I just stood there staring at those dead men. Three days later Curry found me drunk out of my mind in a cheap hotel. I didn't even remember how I got there. I told him

I was finished, done, that I couldn't handle cutting men down in cold blood.''

"What did he say?"

"What you'd expect, I suppose. That I'd only done what I'd had to do, that I was a top-notch agent, my country needed me to continue in my role, the whole nine yards. I bought it because I needed to believe it to save my sanity. That was six years ago. I got tougher, more dangerous assignments, went undercover and didn't surface for months at a time. I pulled the trigger on that gun again and again, and then I lost count. *And every time, it got easier!*''

Unnoticed tears slid down Dawn's cheeks as Creed stopped speaking. He continued to stare at his hands as a chilling silence fell over the room. Seconds, then minutes ticked by. Dawn wanted to pull Creed into her arms, declare her love, offer it as a shield against the horrors of his past. But she didn't move, nor speak.

"About a month ago," Creed said, seemingly unaware of the pause, "Curry showed up and said the two of us had a special, top-priority assignment. The wife of a high-ranking foreign official was being held for ransom, and we were to get her out of the hands of the terrorists. We found them easily enough, because they were three young, stupid hotheads, who didn't know what they were doing. So stupid that they'd killed the wife right after they'd kidnapped her.''

"Dear heaven," Dawn said, "why?"

"I don't know," he said, taking a deep, shuddering breath. "Curry and I came flying through the front door, and he shot two of them as we came in. I stood there, Dawn, with my gun pointed right between that kid's eyes and I froze. He couldn't have been more than eighteen, and he was begging, pleading with me not to shoot him. They hadn't meant to kill the woman, he said, but she'd screamed and one of them had hit her too hard. The kid was sobbing, Curry was yelling something at me, but I couldn't move. Everything just stopped."

Creed got to his feet and walked past Dawn to the window, bracing his hands on the frame.

"I knew at that moment it was over," he said, his voice strained, "because I couldn't figure out what I was doing there. The black tunnel, the emptiness settled over me. The face of every man I had ever killed flashed before my eyes. Killed because I was a killer, and I suddenly didn't know how it had all come to be. I lost myself somewhere, didn't know who I was. I turned and walked out of that room, and the next day I told Curry I was quitting."

"Did he try to talk you out of it?"

"Hell, yes. He said to take a vacation, relax, then I'd be ready to get to work again. He didn't believe I meant it. That's who I was expecting that day I heard the vehicle outside the window. Curry will track me down, try to convince me to come back. I left a trail leading to Greece, then circled around and came home. Came home and started hurting everyone I care about."

"Creed, no," she said, getting to her feet and dropping the doll to the floor. She went to him, circling his waist with her arms and leaning her head on his back. "You haven't hurt anyone except yourself. You believed in what you were doing for your country, but it's over. You can fill the emptiness within you with a new life, purpose. You're not lost. You're Creed Maxwell Parker. And you're home. I don't hate you for what you've done. I love you even more for having the strength to walk away from a life that had become a nightmare for you. I do love you, Creed."

With a strangled moan he turned and pulled her roughly to him, holding her so tightly she could hardly breathe, as he buried his face in the fragrant cloud of her hair.

"I don't know who I am, Dawn," he said, his voice a hoarse whisper.

"You will. Time and trust, remember? You asked them of me, and I agreed. Now you've got to grant yourself the same request. Give yourself time. Trust in yourself, believe." If only he would cry, she thought, her heart aching. He needed to cry, to cleanse his soul. Yes, he was lost, but he had to fight, win, find Creed Parker again. Then, and only then, would there be any hope, any prayer, of his loving her, staying with her.

"I don't deserve you," he said, "but I don't want to let you go. Oh, Dawn, why is it you can accept what I told you, but I can't?"

"You lived it, Creed, I didn't. I can only imagine what those years were like for you. The only part that's real for me is the man I met here on the farm, the man I fell in love with. Nothing you have said has changed how I feel about you."

She lifted her head to smile at him, a warm, tender, loving smile, and Creed's heart thundered in his chest as he gazed down at her.

He hadn't lost his Dawn! his mind repeated over and over. She still loved him! If he declared his love, asked her to marry him, she'd be his forever, his wife, his gift. No! No, he couldn't do that, not yet. Maybe not ever. He'd be taking everything from her, and giving nothing in return. The inner battles were still his to fight. Alone.

"Kiss me, Creed," Dawn whispered. "I really need you to kiss me."

"Dawn," he said, then claimed her mouth.

The kiss was urgent, rough, speaking of Creed's turmoil, anger and frustration. Then slowly it gentled as the taste, the feel, the aroma of the woman in his arms swept the evil forces into a dusty corner of his mind. There was only Dawn. His hands roamed over the material of her robe to come to the sides of her breasts. He filled his palms with their lush fullness as his manhood stirred, strained against his jeans.

"Dawn," he gasped, tearing his mouth from hers.

"Yes?" she asked, taking a shaky breath.

"The word is 'no,'" he said, smiling slightly. "This is hardly the time or the place. But I do want you."

"And I want you, Creed."

"Listen to me," he said, gripping her by the shoulders and moving her away from him. "Even though I've told you what I did, some things haven't changed. I still have nothing to offer you. I can't make plans for my future, until I've dealt with my past."

"I understand."

"I think it would be best if we stayed away from each other for now."

"What?"

"This isn't fair to you. I can't keep taking from you. And I do take, Dawn. I use you to escape from myself. I fill the emptiness with you, warm the aching chill inside of me. No, I'm not going to touch you again until I—"

"Now, you just hold it, Parker!" she interrupted, planting her hands on her hips. Creed's eyebrows shot up in surprise. "I happen to have something to say about this. Your noble gesture stinks!"

"It does?" he said, frowning again.

"Darn right it does! In case you haven't noticed, there is a major battle going on here. I'm up against your past, years of it, with ghosts and horrible memories. That is a formidable opponent, but I have every intention of fighting for you."

"But—"

"Quiet. What you view as wrong, I see as very, very right. I help warm the chill within you? So be it. Ice that melts is gone forever. Quit being so stubborn. There's no law written that says you have to struggle alone. Dark tunnels aren't nearly so frightening when there's someone with you. I'm sticking like glue, Creed Parker, because I love you!"

"Whew!" he said, a smile tugging at his lips. "You're a tough lady."

"You'd better believe it. I'm not standing meekly by, wringing my hands, wondering if you'll ever kiss and hold me again. I might lose, but I intend to put up one heck of a fight!"

"Yeah?" he said, grinning at her.

"Yeah," she replied, folding her arms over her breasts.

He chuckled and shook his head. "You're really something."

"Yes," she said, appearing rather pleased with herself, "I am."

"It's wrong, though," he said, frowning deeply again. "I should work this through alone."

"You're giving me the crazies, Creed Maxwell!" she yelled. "And get your big foot off my doll!"

"What? Oh, sorry," he said, stepping back and picking up the doll. "Hey, this is really cute. I like the freckles."

"Freckles are very popular. I get a lot of orders for freckles."

"You're incredible," he said, placing his hand on her cheek.

"Because I make cute freckles?"

"Yep, and that's not all you have going for you," he said, leaning forward and brushing his lips over hers. "I've got to leave. I'm due at the hospital to see Max."

"Tell him I love him, Creed."

"I will, and I'll speak to whoever is in charge about letting you visit."

"Thank you."

"No, Dawn Gilbert, *I* thank *you*. For everything. I'll see you later."

"'Bye," she said, smiling at him, then turning to watch as he strode from the room. Picking up the doll from the rocker, she ran her fingertip over the freckles she'd sewn on the chubby cheeks. Sudden tears blurred her vision, and she took a wobbly breath. "I can't lose you, Creed," she said to the quiet room. "I can't. I love you too much."

The cardiac care unit was in the form of a circle, with the nurses' station in the center. From that vantage point the monitors above the door to each patient's room could be clearly seen.

Creed entered Max's room and pulled a chair next to the bed, sitting down and gazing at his sleeping father. As if feeling his son's presence, Max slowly lifted his lashes to reveal cloudy blue eyes.

"Hello, Dad," Creed said, smiling. "Fine kettle of fish you've gotten yourself into."

"Did it up right, I guess," Max said, his voice weak.

"Everyone sends their love. Dawn, Elaine, Orv are all thinking about you. Don't worry about the farm. Everything is under control."

"How you doing, Creed?"

"Me? Fine. You're the patient, remember?"

"Creed, I know the truth about you. Have for a long time."

"What?" he said, stiffening in his chair.

"Curry told me."

"He did what?" Creed said, his jaw tightening.

"When your mother was ill, I kept phoning the State Department, but no one seemed to know who you were. Late one night, Curry called."

"We'll talk about this later, Dad," Creed said, covering Max's hand with his. "I don't want you to upset yourself."

"I'm not upset, son. I'm the proudest father in the state of Wisconsin. Curry explained everything. He said he'd find you himself, and get you home as quick as he could."

"Yeah, he came and..." Creed started, his mind racing. Max knew? Had known for five years? Was proud of the fact that his son was a killer? Hell, this didn't make sense! "Dad, I've killed men. I've shot them with a gun that was never inches from my hand."

"I know that, boy. You put your life on the line for this country, for old men like me, for women like Dawn. Curry swore me to secrecy, but I was bursting with pride."

"Why didn't you tell me that you knew?"

"Wasn't my place. I'm only saying it now 'cause I don't know if I have a tomorrow. It's over for you now, isn't it, Creed? You can't do it anymore. I've seen the pain in your eyes. You've twisted what you've done, and turned it on yourself like a knife. Don't do this to yourself, Creed. It's over. Finished. It's time to look ahead to new things, new hopes and dreams.''

"I don't know if I can do that," he said quietly. "I really don't."

"You will. You're a Parker; my son, Jane's son. You're a stubborn, strong-willed man. You'll beat this thing that's haunting you. In the meantime, get me out of this place and take me home."

"Dad, I—"

"Greetings, gentlemen," Dr. North said, coming into the room.

"You're just in time to say goodbye," Max said. "I'm going to my farm."

"That a fact?" the doctor said, chuckling as he flipped through Max's chart.

"That's a fact," Max said.

"In a few days maybe," Dr. North said. "Max, here it is, up front. The tests show your heart is severely damaged. I'll give you medication to control your blood pressure, but that's all I can do. Rest is the key. You can take short, very short, walks but other than that, you sit. Agreed?"

"No," Max said.

"Yes," Creed said.

"Hell's fire," Max muttered.

"If your heart stays stable for the next three days, I'll let you go home. Creed, you're going to have your hands full with this old coot."

"I'm bigger than he is," Creed said. "Don't worry about a thing."

"Five more minutes, Creed," the doctor added. "Then Mr. Personality here has to rest. You can come back tomorrow."

"Doc," Creed said, "those people that were here with me would like to visit Max."

"No can do. The rules here are stricter than San Quentin. Tell your friends to gear up for the arrival of the prisoner. Five minutes," he said, leaving the room.

"Well," Creed said, "you heard the doc."

"I'll do as I please with my own life."

"We'll come to blows about it later. Dad, I don't know what to say to you about you knowing the truth for all these years."

"Then don't say anything. Never could see you in those fancy clothes, sipping tea with your pinkie in the air. I'm a proud father, Creed."

"Thanks, Dad. It's not a big enough word, but it's all I have. I love you very much."

"Fair enough, and I love you. You'll find your peace. I know you will."

"I'll let you rest," Creed said, squeezing his father's hand, then getting to his feet. "I'll see you tomorrow."

"Come back at midnight and sneak me out of here."

"No! Goodbye."

"Hell's fire!"

As Creed emerged from the woods, he saw Orv and waved. The older man stopped and waited for Creed to join him.

"How's Max?" Orv said.

"Ornery."

"Good sign," he said, pulling open the back door. "Elaine, set another place for dinner. Creed's here."

The two men washed their hands, then returned to the kitchen.

"Hello, Creed," Dawn said, smiling at him.

He nodded, then their eyes met and held in a long moment.

"Land's sake," Elaine said, "kiss her, Creed, and be done with it. I can't get this food on the table with the two of you blocking traffic."

"Yes, ma'am," Creed said. He reached for Dawn, bent her backward over his arm and planted a loud smacking kiss on her mouth. "I do everything I'm told," he said, close to her lips.

"Oh, good grief," Dawn said, blushing crimson as Elaine and Orv laughed in delight.

During the meal, Creed brought the Gilberts up to date on Max's condition, telling them the visiting regulations could not be broken.

"Can't see Max just sitting," Orv said, shaking his head.

"My father knows his own mind," Creed said. "He made a decision a year ago when he had that first heart attack, and I'm sure he isn't sorry. I'll caution him to a point about taking it easy, but it's really up to him. No man should be forced to live a life that isn't right for him. Max will decide how he wants to play this."

"He could kill himself if he pushes," Elaine said.

"Then he will have died happy, tending his land. I won't try to stop him. I respect him too much. He granted me that same respect five years ago when he found out I made my living wearing a gun, not a tuxedo."

"Creed!" Dawn said, shock evident on her face.

"He knows, Dawn," Creed said. "Max has known ever since my mother died. He's proud of me. Can you believe that?"

"Yes," she said softly, "I can."

"Elaine, Orv," Creed said, "a few hours ago I snapped at Dawn, said I could never tell you this sitting around the kitchen table, but that's exactly what I'm going to do. It's time you knew the truth."

Dawn sat with her hands clutched tightly in her lap, her eyes riveted on Creed's face as he once again told his story. His voice was flat and low, and she saw the pain flicker across, then settle into his expressive blue eyes. She blinked back her tears, willing herself not to cry.

"God bless you, son," Orv said, when Creed finished speaking.

"My poor boy," Elaine said, dabbing at her eyes with the corner of her apron.

"I chose my own direction, Elaine," Creed said. "The mistake I made was in not turning back before it was too late."

"What will you do now, Creed?" Orv said.

"Take one day at a time for a while. Max needs me, and this time I'm here. I thank you for your understanding. Everyone has been very accepting of what I've done."

"Except you," Dawn said.

"Yeah, well, I'm my own worst enemy, I guess," he said, getting to his feet. "Great dinner, Elaine. Dawn, want to come help me milk the cows?"

"Go," Elaine said. "I'll tend to these dishes. Creed, I'm glad you told us. It explains a lot."

Creed nodded, then extended his hand to Dawn and led her out the back door. In the woods, he pulled her into his arms and kissed her. Dawn circled his neck with her arms and returned the kiss in total abandon, savoring the taste of Creed, his special aroma, the feel of his rugged body pressed to hers.

"So much for never touching you again," Creed said, his breathing ragged.

"I told you it was a lousy idea," she said, trailing her hands slowly down his chest.

"Cows need milking."

"I know," she said, undoing two buttons on his shirt and kissing the moist dark hair on his chest.

"Ah, man," he gasped, "don't do that."

"All is fair in love and war," she said, pushing another button through the hole.

Creed chuckled. "As a very wise man once said, 'Fair enough.' I'll concede this round to you, Miss Gilbert, *after* the cows are milked."

"Fair enough," she said merrily, linking her arm through his. "Shall we go, Farmer Parker?"

The first colorful hues of the summer sunset were streaking across the sky when Creed and Dawn left the barn and made their way through the woods to the swimming hole. There, on the plush carpet of grass, they reached for each other with an urgency that engulfed them both. They kissed and touched until they could bear no more, then became one in a journey of ecstasy. Dawn declared her love for Creed over and over. He whispered his love for her in his mind.

Sated, they lay quietly, close, allowing the tranquillity of the setting to cloak them in contentment.

"Elaine and Orv aren't blind," Creed said finally. "I'm sure they know there's something happening between you and me. They might not approve after what I told them."

"Don't be silly," Dawn said, snuggling closer to him. "They love you, Creed. If they're concerned, it's for you. They knew something was wrong the minute you arrived home."

"Remind me never to play poker. I'm apparently very transparent."

"It's your eyes. Your eyes mirror your feelings."

"Oh, yeah?" he said, rolling on top of her. "And what do you see?"

"Shame on you! That's a very naughty message you're delivering."

"And?" he said, lowering his mouth to hers.

"I accept delivery."

Much later, Creed escorted Dawn through the woods, kissed her deeply, then waited until she was safely inside the house. He returned to the back steps of the Parker home and sat down, watching the fireflies dance through the darkness. The events of the day replayed in his mind, and settled over him in a heavy depression.

The term "odd man out," applied to him, he thought. He was surrounded by people who fully accepted, seemingly understood, the path he'd chosen for his life. Proud, his father had stated adamantly. Proud of his son who killed. Once, whenever it was, Creed, too, had registered a sense of pride at serving his country in such a specialized, crucial role. He'd rationalized it all with a sense of patriotism. Then it had all caught up with him. The devil had wanted his due. And, oh, Lord, how dearly Creed was paying.

Creed took a deep breath, filling his lungs with air, inhaling the scents of the farm. Rich scents, earthy, real. Tomorrow he'd finish plowing the field, he decided, then start painting the house before driving to Madison in the afternoon to see Max. In a few days he'd bring his father home to this land. Then he'd step back and allow Max to make the choice whether or not to follow the doctor's orders. Out of love and respect, Creed would leave him alone to make the decision.

As quickly as the depression had crept over Creed, it disappeared. He had a full day ahead of him tomorrow, he realized. A productive day, with a sense of purpose that would produce visible evidence of his labors. And tomorrow would start with the beauty of a dawn, and with *his* Dawn. His lovely, wonderful Dawn.

For the first time since Creed could remember, he felt a sense of anticipation for the new day ahead.

"Damn it, pig, back up," Creed said. "I can't get to the trough to feed you when you're leaning against me! Move!"

Creed stiffened as he heard a noise in the woods, then relaxed as Dawn emerged waving and smiling at him.

That was all the pig needed.

As Creed raised his arm to return Dawn's greeting, the hog leaned its two hundred pounds farther into Creed's knees.

"Oh, good Lord!" Creed yelled, then down he went, flat on his back in the mud. The expletives that reached Dawn's ears were very colorful.

"Well, hi!" she said brightly, climbing up on the fence and peering at Creed. "How's life?"

"Damn it!" he said, struggling to his feet in the slime.

"That good, huh?" she said, her laughter bubbling through the air. "I missed you at the swimming hole this morning. There I was, naked as a jaybird, with no one to keep me company. Such a shame. I don't think mud is your color, Creed. It's rather icky, you know what I mean?"

"Zip it, Gilbert," he growled, sloshing to the trough and dumping in the bucket of slop. "Damn it, pig, move!"

"I think she likes you."

"Pork chops and bacon," he said. "Hear that, hog? And thick ham sandwiches. And sausage!"

Dawn dissolved in a fit of laughter.

"I'm warning you, Dawn! Knock it off!" Creed roared.

"It's just so-o-o funny! You should see yourself."

Creed turned and advanced toward her, arms raised, hands curled into clawlike fists. He walked stiff-kneed like a robot, growling ferociously.

"Oh, no!" Dawn said, jumping down from the fence. "Don't you touch me with that mud on you! Don't you dare, Creed Parker!"

"Grrr! Kiss me!" he rumbled.

"No way!" she said, taking off at a run toward the house.

Creed put his hand on top of the fence and vaulted over in a smooth motion, sprinting forward the second his feet hit the ground.

Dawn didn't stand a chance.

Large muddy hands gripped her waist, spun her around and flattened her against a rock-hard body.

"Oh, blak!" she said. "Oh, yuck!"

"You're so articulate," Creed said, then kissed her very thoroughly.

"Just look at my clothes!" she shrieked, when Creed finally released her. "The kiss was super but, darn it, I'm a mess!"

"No problem," he said, grabbing her by the hand and hauling her across the lawn. "I'll fix you right up. What we need here is a little water."

"Bad plan," Dawn said, attempting to dig her heels into the grass to halt her flight. "Terrible. Not good. I'll go home and take a shower."

"I wouldn't hear of it," he said, grinning at her. "I always clean up the messes I make. And you are definitely a mess."

Creed turned on the faucet, picked up the hose and drenched a sputtering Dawn from head to foot.

"Give me that," she said, snatching the hose from him. "Now it's my turn."

"Be my guest," he said, holding out his arms. "I'll just stand here and enjoy the view."

"The what?" she said, then glanced down at herself. The thin material of her wet blouse clung to her breasts, outlining them to perfection. The buds grew taut under Creed's scrutiny, and a burst of laughter escaped from her lips. "How much did you pay the pig to knock you over?"

"Ten bucks. It's worth every penny."

"There's a name for people like you."

"Innovative. Brilliant. Then there's— Aaagh! That's wet! And cold!"

"Close your mouth before you drown. Hey, this is fun!"

And it *was* fun. Their laughter intermingled and sparkled through the air. The hose managed to change ownership several times, until Creed finally turned off the faucet. He lifted Dawn off her feet and held her high on his chest.

"You're so good for me," he said. "You make me laugh right out loud."

"I love you, Creed," she said, then lowered her lips to his.

He slid her slowly, sensuously down his body, their lips never parting. When her feet reached the grass, his hands moved to nestle her against him, to feel the hard evidence of his arousal.

"But you just had a cold shower," she said breathlessly.

"Tells you how much cold showers are worth," he murmured, trailing a ribbon of kisses down her neck.

"Oh, Creed," she said, desire swirling throughout her.

"Right," he said, stepping slowly away from her. "Duty and chores call."

"Yes, I have to get back, too. I promised Elaine I'd pick the raspberries. I came over here to ask you if I could ride into Madison with you. I need to deliver an order of dolls to a shop there."

"Great. I wish they'd let you visit Max."

"So do I."

"I'll pick you up about two. Well, I'm off to plow the field."

"Soaking wet? You'll be a mudpie again."

"Know anyone who might volunteer to hose me down?"

"Nope."

"Kiss me, Gilbert."

"Oh, Parker, how can I resist such a romantic request?" she said, slipping her arms around his neck.

"That wasn't romantic? What if I said 'please'? Please kiss me. Please take off your clothes. Please ravish my body until I'm too weak to move."

"Go plow a field," she said, then kissed him. "Now, I've got to go home," she said, taking a deep breath as she slid her hands down his wet shirt. "I'll see you at two."

"I'll be counting the hours, minutes and seconds," he said, covering his heart with his hand.

"Now that was romantic. See ya."

Creed watched as Dawn hurried toward the woods. He whooped with laughter when he heard her parting words.

"Thanks, pig," she called. "You just became my best friend!"

Seven

Creed folded his arms over his chest and nodded in approval. He'd finished painting half of the front of the house, and it looked good. The blue was a perfect color, blending into the setting. Max, he hoped, would be pleased.

A half hour later, Creed had showered, then dressed in dark slacks and a yellow shirt open at the neck. He slid behind the wheel of Max's truck and drove to the Gilbert farm to pick up Dawn. He parked in front, shouted a greeting as he entered the living room, then stopped in his tracks.

"Good Lord," he muttered, as the blood pounded through his veins.

Dawn had halted halfway down the stairs, her hand resting on the banister. Her white dress was a peasant style made of gauzy material, with brightly embroidered flowers at the scooped neckline and around the

hem. Her three-inch heels accentuated the gentle slope
of her calves. Coral ribbons had been interwoven
through her hair, which was braided, then coiled onto
the top of her head.

Creed cleared his throat roughly. "You are the most
beautiful woman I have ever seen," he said, his voice
slightly gritty. "You are lovelier than the dawn and
sunset combined. There aren't enough words to de-
scribe... Well..." His voice trailed off, and he appeared slightly embarrassed as he shoved his hands
into his pockets.

Dawn moved gracefully down the remaining steps,
a soft smile on her face as she stopped in front of him,
placing her hands on his cheeks.

"Thank you," she said, then said no more, as her
throat tightened.

They stood, not moving, each seeming to memo-
rize the moment, etch it indelibly in their minds. The
warmth from Dawn's fingertips sent whispers of heat
throughout Creed, igniting his desire. He kept his
hands in his pockets, fists tightly clenched, as he re-
sisted the urge to pull Dawn into his arms and bring his
mouth down hard onto hers. He was acutely aware of
his own strength, and the fragile beauty of her lissome body. His manhood stirred with the need, the
want, to bury himself deep within her honeyed femininity. But he didn't move.

Dawn tilted her head slightly to the side, an expression of near-wonder on her face, almost awe. She
moved her fingers over Creed's face in a feathery ex-
ploration of his rugged, tanned features, tracing each
in turn. She inhaled his fresh soapy scent which was
the mingling of a woodsy after-shave with an aroma
that was simply male. She anticipated the sensual

pleasure of tasting him, feeling his mouth on hers, the sweet torture of his tongue dueling with hers. Her breasts grew heavy, aching for his tantalizing touch. The coil of need deep within her ignited a rambling flame of passion throughout her.

Dawn sighed, marveling at the beauty of this man, marveling at the intensity of her love for him. They weren't even touching, except for the tips of her fingers, and he excited her like no man before.

She slid her hands to his shoulders, feeling the muscles tremble under her foray. His sharp intake of breath matched the discovery of his male nipples beneath her palms as her hands moved lower.

"Dawn," he gasped, "you're driving me crazy!"

"You are so beautiful," she said, then pressed her mouth to his.

Creed's hands whipped out of his pockets to grip her upper arms. He hauled her against him, his mouth crushing hers. Dawn moaned in pleasure, returning the kiss in total abandon, savoring every sensation that rocketed through her. She leaned into him, relishing his heat, his strength, the power within him that he held in check.

Creed struggled for control as he felt himself slipping into oblivion. Dear Lord, how he wanted this woman! He would kiss every inch of her velvety skin, bring her to a height of passion never before experienced. Nothing would exist but the two of them, and the ecstasy of their union.

"Dawn!" he said, tearing his mouth from Dawn's. "We're in Elaine and Orv's living room!"

What did that have to do with anything? Dawn thought dreamily, slowly lifting her lashes. So what if they were . . .

"Oh, dear heaven," she said.

"Man," Creed said, running his hand down his face, "another minute and it would have been too late. What you do to me is unbelievable."

"Dawn?" Elaine called from the kitchen. "Did I hear Creed drive up?"

"Oh, Lord," Creed said, grabbing Dawn by the shoulders and spinning her around. He placed her directly in front of him, her back to him, his hands resting on her shoulders.

"What are you doing?" Dawn said, her breathing not yet steady. "Are we posing for a picture?"

He chuckled. "I certainly hope not."

Creed pressed against her, and Dawn's eyes widened as she felt his manhood.

"Well, there you are," Elaine said, bustling into the room.

"Yes, we certainly are," Dawn said, then giggled. Creed groaned.

"Are you leaving for Madison now?" Elaine said.

"No!" they said in unison.

"In a minute or so," Creed said. "I think. I hope."

"You'll have dinner with us, won't you, Creed?" Elaine said. "I'm making raspberry cobbler for dessert."

"Thank you," he said. "Sounds great."

"Creed will be ready for a good meal," Dawn said. "He's had a *hard* day."

"I'm going to wring your neck," he muttered under his breath. She giggled again.

"Fine," Elaine said. "Well, have a nice trip into town, and give Max our love."

"See ya," Creed said, as Elaine hurried back to her kitchen. "Let's get the hell out of here," he growled, striding to the door.

Dawn laughed merrily as she picked up her purse and a large shopping bag containing her dolls. Creed was already behind the wheel of the truck, and she slid in next to him, placing the bag against the door.

"I feel like a fifteen-year-old kid who got caught kissin' in the parlor," he said. He turned the key roughly in the ignition and drove away from the house, a stormy expression on his face. "I need, I want, to make love to you, Dawn Gilbert! I'm going to pull off the road and take you in a damn corn field!"

"Goodness, how very bohemian."

He shot her a dark glare, then a slow smile crept onto his face, finally erupting into laughter. "This is crazy," he said, serious again. "We're adults, not children. I want you in my bed, Dawn. I want to make love to you at night, and wake up next to you in the morning."

Then marry me, you dunderhead! Dawn thought. Should she say that out loud? No, it was definitely beyond her scope of liberation. Creed had never even said that he loved her. Those precious words had never been spoken by him.

"We have other people to consider, Creed," she said. "I can't just pack up and move in with you."

"I know," he said, sighing deeply. "But, damn it, I was milking cows this morning while you were at the swimming hole. When, where, are we going to make love?"

"Do you really hate having to do those chores?"

"What? Oh, no, not at all. It feels good tending the farm. There's a reason, a purpose, for everything a man does. I got half of the front of the house painted, too."

"I'm supposed to help you!"

"There's plenty left to do, believe me. The blue is great. Nice color. Once I reach an understanding with that pig, I'll have everything under control."

"Then you're enjoying what you're doing?"

"Yeah, I said I was. Am I being interviewed?"

"No, but when you came home I don't imagine you expected to take over running the farm. I just wondered how you felt about it. It's a very different lifestyle."

"From what I was doing? True. The farm is proving to be exactly what I need right now."

Right now, Dawn's mind echoed. Swell. But what about the future, the forevers? Did Creed envision himself as a farmer for the rest of his life? Everything was in limbo, a twilight zone. He was a prisoner of his past, functioning in the present in a role his father needed him to be in. But what would tomorrow bring? He wanted her to be his lover. Her dreams encompassed marriage, children, life on the farm together.

"You're awfully quiet all of a sudden," Creed said, glancing over at her.

"Things are very complicated at the moment. So much has happened very quickly."

"Yes, the good with the bad. You are on the top of the good list. Things will smooth out once Max comes home. This dashing into Madison every day isn't normal. I'll get a routine worked out that will definitely include some private time for you and me. Somehow. I would have liked to stay in Madison and take you to dinner, but I have to milk the cows. I'm such a dedicated farmer," he said, chuckling softly.

But for how long? Dawn's mind screamed. Oh, enough of this. She was going to totally depress herself. She had Creed all to herself for the next few hours, and she intended to enjoy!

"How does this sound?" Creed asked. "Instead of splitting up, you come to the hospital with me. They don't let me stay very long. Then we'll go deliver your dolls together. Treat me right, and I'll buy you an ice cream soda."

"Fantastic," she said, her buoyant mood restored. "I adore ice cream sodas."

"And I adore you. Lord, what a dumb word. You're turning me into a romantic."

Dawn laughed, then leaned her head on Creed's shoulder. Her distressing thoughts were pushed away, and a smile stayed on her lips during the remaining miles into Madison.

At the hospital, Dawn settled onto a leather chair in the waiting room after telling Creed to give Max a big hug from her. A few minutes later, Dr. North came in.

"Dawn Gilbert?" he said.

"Yes," she said, getting quickly to her feet.

"I know when I'm outnumbered. I'll give you five minutes with Max. If anyone asks, you're a heart specialist from Burbank or wherever."

"Oh, thank you! How is Max doing?"

"Much better than I'd hoped or expected. He's a tough old bird. He also lights up like a church whenever he speaks of Creed. I take it that Creed just arrived home?"

"Yes, he was away for many years."

"Well, he's the best medicine there is for Max. A patient's mental attitude can have a great deal to do with their recovery. I hope Creed plans on sticking around."

"I'm not really sure," Dawn said quietly. "He's just taking one day at a time for now."

"That's understandable under the circumstances. This situation with Max is shaky. Although, if he follows my orders, I think he has a good chance of coming through this."

"Max is stubborn. His farm is his life, his world. Creed feels that Max has the right to make his own decisions."

"That's true," the doctor said, nodding. "Well, time will tell. Go give the old buzzard a big kiss. Third door on the right."

"Thank you again. I've been so worried about him. I really appreciate your letting me see him."

"Max is a lucky man to have such loving family and friends. 'Bye for now."

Everyone was interested in Creed's plans, Dawn thought ruefully, as she walked down the hall. The frightening part was, she didn't think Creed himself knew. He might wake up one morning and decide it was time for him to move on. Would he really do that? Just pack up and go? Leave her? Well, why not? He'd never said he loved her. Smile, she told herself firmly. Smile for Max.

"Hello," she said, poking her head in the door.

"There's my little girl," Max said. "Come in, come in."

Dawn walked to the edge of the bed and hugged him. "Oh, Max, I was so worried," she said, "but you look wonderful. You're probably just staying here to bat your beautiful blue eyes at the nurses."

"I'm bored with that, so take me home."

"Here he goes again," Creed said, rolling his eyes.

"You'll be home soon, Max," Dawn said, taking his hand in hers. "The raspberries are ready to pick, and Elaine is starting out with cobbler, with lots of goodies to come."

"Raspberry jam," Max said, "on homemade bread. Sounds mighty good to me. All I've had in this place is Jell-o and watered-down soup."

"Well," Creed said, "get used to less than fancy meals, Dad. I just became the chief cook at the Parker farm, and my culinary expertise consists of very strong coffee."

Max chuckled. "You used to make a pretty decent peanut butter sandwich when you were a boy."

"I can probably still stick one of those together," Creed said, smiling. "You'll have to view this as an experience."

"If my heart doesn't get me, the cooking will. As long as I'm back on my farm, I won't complain."

"Won't be long," Creed said, getting to his feet. "Our time is up. I'll see you tomorrow."

"Goodbye, Max," Dawn said, kissing him on the cheek. "Behave yourself."

"Goodbye, Dawn. You're pretty as a picture in that dress. You look like a bride."

"Save your blarney for the nurses," she said, laughing. "See you soon."

"'Bye, Dad," Creed said. "I'll spring you from this joint as quickly as possible."

"Fair enough," Max said.

Pretty as a bride, Dawn thought, as she and Creed walked down the hall. Now all she needed was a groom. Maybe she'd whop Creed over the head and drag him to the courthouse.

"Max looks good, don't you think?" Creed said in the elevator.

"Yes, he really does. His color is normal, and he's certainly feisty. Creed, do you think he'll disregard the doctor's orders once he's home?"

"I don't know," he said quietly. "Max is the only one who can decide about that."

"Yes," she said frowning, "I suppose so."

"Hey, one day at a time, remember?"

"Okay. Listen, there's no reason for you to cook. Elaine makes tons of food every day. I'll pack a basket and bring it over to you and Max. Or I could do the meals right at your house. I'm very good in the kitchen, but Elaine loves to cook so I don't get much of a chance."

"No, I don't think that's a good idea."

"Why not?"

"I can't ask you or Elaine to take that on. Max and I will muddle through. I'll get the hang of cooking. It can't be all that tough. Where to, Miss Dawn's Dolls?" Creed said, as they walked outside.

Dawn absently gave Creed the directions to the boutique she needed to go to, then climbed into the truck. Her feelings were hurt, she realized. She *wanted* to prepare Creed and Max's meals, move around in that kitchen, provide for the Parker men. It would be like playing house, pretending she and Creed were married and she really belonged there. But independent, stubborn Creed, was going to do it all himself. Perhaps the thought of her functioning in that role made him uncomfortable, presented a picture of a little wife in the kitchen, and he wanted no part of that scenario. Well, fine! She hoped his peanut sandwiches stuck to the roof of his mouth!

"So there!" she said.

"What's your problem?" Creed said, as he maneuvered the truck through the traffic.

She burst into laughter. "I'm just throwing a mental tantrum," she said. "I'd really like to cook for you and Max, and since I didn't get my own way, I'm pouting."

"Dawn, try to understand. I'm so afraid that I'll allow myself to concentrate only on you, and not the problems I have to deal with. You would look so right in that house cooking meals the way Elaine does in hers. I could get caught up in the fantasy and never face reality. Look, if it turns out that I'm close to poisoning Max, I'll reconsider. Okay?"

"Okay," she said, smiling brightly. Creed *did* see her cooking for him in his home. It wasn't that he didn't want her there, it went back to that damnable past of his. Well, he was going to get a handle on all of that. Oh, dear heaven, he just had to!

The boutique was in an affluent section of Madison, and was one of several small shops situated around a grassy area with trees and a fountain.

"Megabuck folks," Creed said, as they approached the store.

"Yes. You wouldn't believe what they charge for my dolls. It's ridiculous, but you'll notice that I don't object when they hand me my check. Are you coming in?"

"Sure. I want to see you in action, high roller. Besides, I'm carrying the babies."

In the boutique, Dawn was greeted by a pleasant woman in her forties named Gwen. Dawn introduced her to Creed, then presented Gwen with the new supply of dolls.

"And here is your check for the others," Gwen said. "They sold in ten days. I could use twice what you bring me. Oh, here he comes. Dawn, that man walking across the courtyard wants to see you. I told him you'd be in this afternoon, and he said he'd be back."

"Who is he?" Dawn asked.

Before Gwen could reply, the man entered the store. He was dressed in an obviously expensive three-piece suit, and had perfectly groomed gray hair.

"Good timing, Mr. Matts," Gwen said. "This is Dawn Gilbert of Dawn's Dolls, and Creed Parker."

"Paul Matts," he said, smiling and shaking hands with Dawn, then Creed. "I was hoping to have a word with you, Miss Gilbert. Perhaps we could go out under the trees and sit on one of those benches."

Dawn glanced at Creed, but he had no readable expression on his face. Apparently, he was not going to step into her world of Dawn's Dolls.

"What did you wish to speak to me about, Mr. Matts?" she asked.

"It's Paul," he said. "Shall we go outside?"

"Well, I guess so. Goodbye, Gwen. See you soon. Creed?"

"I can wait in the truck."

"No, please join us," Dawn said.

"All right," Creed said. Matts was in his early fifties, he mused. Tan was natural, not a sunlamp number. Loose gait. Athlete. Kept himself in good shape. And he was loaded with money, according to the sheen on the suit, the well-groomed haircut, the quality of his watch. So, what did the hotshot want with Dawn?

"Miss Gilbert," Paul Matts said, after the three were seated on a bench, "I own a promotion firm here in Madison, with branch offices in Milwaukee and Chicago. My secretary purchased one of your dolls, and the other women in the office were enchanted with it. My professional ears perked up, and I did some investigating, which led to you. The whole concept of Dawn's Dolls is marvelous, and I congratulate you on producing a unique and very marketable product."

"Well, thank you," Dawn said.

Smooth, Creed thought. Very smooth. The guy had class.

"What I would like to do," Paul continued, "is promote you through my firm. I know that each of your dolls is handmade, and no two are alike. I don't wish to tamper with that at all. What I'm talking about is an extension of Dawn's Dolls in the form of a line of little girl's clothing, lunch boxes, dishes—the list is endless."

"Good heavens," Dawn said.

"And then, there's the promotion of you."

"I beg your pardon?" Dawn said.

Here it comes, Creed thought, frowning.

"Gwen told me that you were a pretty young woman," Paul said, "but that hardly describes you. You're very beautiful."

"Oh, well, thank you," she said, smiling slightly.

Brother! Creed thought, shifting his weight and deepening his frown.

"The American people love a success story," Paul said. "Here you are, a lovely woman living on a farm, sewing your dolls, and suddenly you're a highly successful businesswoman. I can get you on talk shows, interviewed by top magazines, newspapers, all of which will further promote the Dawn's Dolls products. I can also see autograph sessions across the country, where the little girls will want to meet Dawn herself. It will call for very careful planning and timing, but I assure you I know how to do it. My reputation speaks for itself. We both stand to make a great deal of money, plus you'll gain public recognition."

"Oh, Mr. Matts, Paul, I really don't think I—"

"Don't give me your answer today," he interrupted. "Here's my card. I realize I hit you with a great deal at once, and you need to think it over. I'll expect to hear from you within the next two weeks. You're welcome to have your attorney examine our contract before you sign it. We want you to be comfortable with us, Miss Gilbert. I can guarantee you a very lucrative and exciting future. I'll wait to hear from you," he said, getting to his feet.

Dawn and Creed also stood, and handshakes were exchanged. As Paul Matts walked away, Dawn sank back onto the bench and stared at the card in her hand. Creed leaned his shoulder against a tree and crossed his arms over his chest. A muscle twitched in his tightly clenched jaw.

Damn it! he thought. Dawn had just been offered the world on a silver platter! Money, travel, everything. *And* recognition for something that she had accomplished on her own, that was totally hers. This was her ticket off the farm, a chance at an exciting new life she'd created, earned. But, ah, no! He didn't want her to do this! Yet he sure didn't have the right to say a word. He loved her, but couldn't tell her. Wanted to marry her, but couldn't ask her. He had to keep his mouth shut!

"Did that really happen?" Dawn asked, shaking her head. "This is unbelievable."

"You can check the guy out, but I'd say he's on the level. So? What do you think?" Creed said, keeping a casual tone in his voice.

Dawn looked up at him quickly, shock evident on her face. "I wouldn't even consider it, Creed."

"Why not?" he said, pulling a leaf from the tree and studying it. "It's a wingding offer."

"I lived in the fast lane once, remember?" she said, getting to her feet. "I hated it."

"That was your parents' world and money. This is different. You've done this on your own, and you'd be in charge of things. Matts can't force you to do anything you don't want to. Where you went, what you did, would be up to you."

"You sound as though you want me to do this," she said. Oh, no, she thought. What about them? Their future together? Did he really want her to pack up and go to a glitsy world, leave the farm? Leave him? Maybe so. After all, he'd never said that *he* was staying on the farm. And he'd never said he loved her.

"It's not my place to express an opinion," he said, lifting his shoulders in a shrug, as he tore the leaf into small pieces. "It's like this thing with Max. You have to make your own choices regarding your life. We all do. The bottom line is, it's up to you."

"I see," she said quietly, sudden tears prickling at the back of her eyes. "You're right, of course. It's my life to do with as I choose. However," she said, her voice trembling slightly, "I would think that the fact

that I love you would play some importance in my
plans for the future."

Every muscle in Creed's body tightened as his heart
pounded in his chest. A trickle of sweat ran down his
back as he forced himself to concentrate on shredding
the leaf. There were tears in Dawn's voice, and he
didn't dare look at her, see the hurt and confusion he
knew would be in her eyes. He wanted to rage in anger, shout at her, tell her she was his, and he loved her.
He loved her and she wasn't going anywhere without
him!

But he couldn't say those things, because he hadn't
earned the right to declare his love. He had felt the
beginning of a small sense of peace within himself as
he'd labored on the farm, but it wasn't enough. He
wasn't healed, whole, complete. He was less than a
total man, and Dawn deserved better. Maybe, just
maybe, the farm and its way of life were to be his sal-
vation. But he didn't know yet!

"Creed?"

"Matts offered you a hell of a lot," he said, dusting off his hands. "I have *nothing* to offer you." He
turned slowly to face her, his muscles actually aching
from tension. "Want that ice cream soda now?"

"Do I want an ice cream soda?" she said, an in-
credulous expression on her face. "Doesn't it matter
to you that I could leave the farm? Doesn't my love
mean anything at all? Your one-day-at-a-time philos-
ophy works very well for you, doesn't it? Provided, of
course, there's some sex thrown in to each of those
days!"

"Damn it, don't talk like that!" he said.

"I don't think it would bother you one iota if I accepted Matts's offer," she said, her voice rising. "I

could write letters home about the fancy places I'd seen, but at least mine would be true! You got very good at lying, didn't you, Creed? You told me how much you care for me, how happy you are that I came into your life, and I believed every word. I can understand your hands-off policy in regard to Max. But I can't understand a man who claims to have deep feelings for a woman, who would stand silently by and watch her walk out of his life!"

"He does it," Creed said, his voice low as he drew a shuddering breath, "if he has no right to ask her to stay."

"No right? Or no reason? There's a tremendous difference between the two. Which is it, Creed?"

"I've had enough of this," he said tightly. "Let's go home."

"Answer me! Which is it?"

No right! his mind screamed. But to say it out loud, at that moment, would sway her decision regarding Matts's offer. That answer would give her the hope that he would beat the insidious ghosts of his past and come to her. That answer asked for more time and trust from her, with no guarantees as to the outcome. That answer wasn't fair to her; it wasn't his to give.

And so Creed said nothing.

He knew how well Dawn could see the pain in his eyes, so he shoved his hands into his pockets and stared at the ground. And said nothing. The knife of loneliness twisted in his gut, the dark tunnel moved in around him, the emptiness screamed at him in a multitude of voices. Sweat poured down his back and chest, as a cadence beat unmercifully against his temples. Seconds ticked by, each measuring a greater distance between him and the woman he loved. His precious gift. His Dawn.

Dawn stared at him, mentally begging him to say he wanted her to stay with him, but felt he had no right to ask it of her. He *did* have the right, because she loved him, would put him first, forsaking all others and all things. But that love had to mean something to Creed. It had to touch his soul, his heart, his mind. His silence beat against her, caused unnoticed tears to spill onto her cheeks, spoke volumes with its stillness.

She had lost.

Whatever ember of caring he'd had for her had been crushed into dust by the heavy burden of his past. And he *had* cared for her. Her harsh words accusing him of lying to her about his feelings had been spoken in anger, without thought. What they had been building together had been real and honest. But it had been put to the test before its time, before the present could outweigh the past, then grant them a future.

What Creed had reached for so tentatively with her, he was now retreating from, refusing to pay credence to. He stood alone again, enclosed in the unyielding walls of his dark tunnel. She loved him, but it hadn't been enough to win the battle.

She had lost.

"I'd like to go home, please," she said, her voice no more than a whisper.

Creed nodded, then walked slightly behind her as they went to the truck. The drive back to the Gilbert farm was made in silence; icy, heavy silence. Dawn glanced down at her pretty dress, registering an irrational feeling of amazement that she was still wearing it, that this was the same day she had walked down the stairs in the warm glow of Creed's appreciative gaze.

They had stood there in a moment that had held greater awareness, discovery, an increasing intensity of what they shared. And now it was over, splintered into a million pieces and whisked into oblivion, leaving no trace but the ache in her heart.

In front of the Gilbert house, Creed stopped the truck but didn't turn off the ignition.

"Tell Elaine thank-you," he said, his voice flat, "but I'll start practicing my cooking tonight."

"Yes, of course," Dawn said tightly, opening the door.

"Dawn, I..." he started, then stopped speaking.

"Yes?" she said, not turning to look at him.

"Nothing."

A few moments later the front door banged behind her as Dawn ran into the house.

"Nothing," he said to no one, "except I love you and I'm sorry. I do love you, Dawn."

He drove home slowly, then walked up the stairs to his bedroom with dragging steps. He changed into old jeans, then went back outside. There, until it was time to milk the cows, he blanked his mind and painted. He painted the house the delicate shade of blue that matched Dawn's satin ribbon.

Eight

Ah, man!'' Creed said, waving his arms in the air to clear away the smoke. "That's not an egg, it's a hockey puck!"

"Good morning," Elaine said, coming in the back door. "Call the fire department yet?"

"Cute. The first three eggs were runny. The last three were bricks. The hell with it. I'll have pie and coffee."

"Would you settle for warm biscuits?" she asked, handing him a basket covered with a towel.

"You're a sweetheart," he said, pouring a cup of coffee, then sitting down at the table.

Elaine scraped out the frying pan, then broke four eggs into it.

"Dawn told us about Paul Matts last night," she said.

"I assumed she would."

"She said you feel it's her decision to make alone."

"That's right," he said, starting on his second biscuit.

"Mmm."

Creed waited for Elaine to speak again, glancing over at her where she stood by the stove. She placed a plate of eggs in front of him, refilled his coffee cup, then loaded the dishwasher. When she had filled the sink with hot sudsy water, he'd had enough of her brand of silence.

"Damn it!" he shouted, smacking the table with his hand. "Knock it off!"

"I haven't said a word," she said calmly, scouring the frying pan.

"You can say more by not saying anything than anyone I know," he said, none too quietly.

"That didn't make a bit of sense. But then, what should I expect coming from a man who doesn't make a bit of sense at all? I thought Max was stubborn, but you take the cake, Creed Maxwell. It will be the comeuppence you deserve the day Dawn packs her bags and goes traipsing across the country with that Paul Matts."

"Like hell she will!" he roared, instantly on his feet.

"Mmm."

"Where is she?" he yelled.

"Tending her chickens."

The screen door hummed on its hinges due to the force with which Creed slammed it as he went barreling out, heading for the woods at full speed. Elaine lifted the frying pan for inspection, and the shiny surface reflected her wide smile.

Dawn placed the sixth egg in the sling she had made with the bottom of her cotton blouse. She cradled her arm beneath her fragile cargo as though nestling a baby below her breasts. After bidding her clucking friends adieu, she stepped out of the enclosure and latched the gate.

"Dawn!" a deep voice bellowed.

As she turned, her eyes widened when she saw Creed thundering toward her. His expression was as menacing as a winter storm, and her eyes grew even wider.

"I want to talk to you," he said, pulling up short in front of her. "Right now!"

"Goodness, you must be in excellent shape. You ran all that way, and you're not even winded," she said, smiling up at him.

"Dawn!"

"Oh. What was it you wished to speak to me about, Creed?"

"Matts. And his Dawn's Dolls's ideas," he said, volume on high. "Do you really want a picture of your dolls on a lunch box? Do you? Do you want to live out of suitcases, sleep in sleazy hotels?"

"Sleazy?"

"Yeah, sleazy! There are users, takers, out there, Dawn. Everyone will want a cut of the pie, some of the action. It's cutthroat big business, and no one will give a damn that you're the most trusting, the most wonderful woman on the face of the earth. You'll be in a hot tub, instead of the natural beauty of a swimming hole where you belong!"

"Well, I—"

"And furthermore," he continued, beginning to pace back and forth with heavy strides, "I don't want you to go! I have no right—catch that?—no *right* to say a word, but I have to, or I'll pop a gasket. Aren't you happy on the farm? Yes, damn it, you are! Any idiot can tell that. You belong here, Dawn. This is the world for you, not the flash and dash that Matts is dangling under your nose.''

"But—"

"Would you just listen?" he shouted, stopping in front of her.

"Yes, of course," she said, nodding solemnly. "But do you have to holler?"

"Yes! You think I don't have a *reason* for wanting you here? Wrong! I do! I love you, Dawn Gilbert! I love you!''

Dawn gasped, then a lovely smile came to her lips as she gazed up at a scowling Creed.

"You do?" she asked, her voice hushed. "You love me, Creed?"

"I didn't mean to say that," he muttererd. "But, yes!" he went on, yelling again. "Yes, I do! Ah, the hell with it," he growled, then hauled her up against him and brought his mouth down hard onto hers.

Eggs have never been known for the durability of their shells.

As Dawn was crushed to Creed's body, so went the eggs. Her eyes shot open and she stiffened in his arms as a crackling noise reverberated through the air, and a warm, sticky substance began to soak through her blouse.

"What in the..." Creed started, then his mouth dropped open as he looked down.

Dawn drew her arm away and as if in slow motion the eggs, slightly scrambled, slid off the material, landing with a plop on the top of Creed's shoes. Neither Dawn nor Creed moved. They simply stood there, staring at the gooey mess as though they had never seen an egg before in their entire lives.

"I can't believe this," Creed said, shaking his head. "This isn't happening to me. I tell the only woman I have ever loved that I love her, and it turns into a situation comedy."

"This is the most romantic, the most wonderful moment of my life," Dawn said, flinging her arms around his neck and molding herself to him. "Oh, dear," she said, an instant later, jumping back. "Now I've gotten eggs on your shirt and jeans!"

"They'll wash. Come here, Dawn," he said softly. "I really do need to kiss you."

Forgotten were the eggs, the eggshells and the condition of their clothes. Forgotten were the hurt and confusion of the previous day, and the long, sleepless night both had endured. There was only the kiss. Sensuous and sweet, then deepening in its intensity as their tongues met, the kiss took their breath away. It spoke of love, and trust, and commitment. It heightened their passion, caused heartbeats to quicken, and pulses to skitter. It went on and on. It was Dawn and Creed held tightly in each other's arms, oblivious to anything other than the one they loved. The kiss was sensational!

"Good Lord," Creed said, taking a ragged breath, "first in a living room, now by a chicken coop. One of these days I'll really forget where I am when I'm kissing you and land in jail."

"Please say it again," Dawn whispered. "Tell me that you love me."

He cradled her face in his large hands. "Oh, Dawn, I do love you so very much. I didn't feel I had the right to tell you, I still don't. Look, we need to talk. Have you finished your chores?"

"I certainly have," she said, peering down at her blouse.

"Go change, and I'll hose myself off. We'll walk down to the swimming hole."

"Which is so much nicer than a hot tub," she said, smiling at him. "I'll be right back."

Ah, man, Creed thought, watching Dawn run to the house, what had he done? Some secret agent *he* was. He'd just spilled the beans about something he'd had no intention of making known. But oh, what a beautiful glow had come to Dawn's face, such happiness had shown in her eyes when he'd said that he loved her. He had brought her that joy. Him! Creed Maxwell Parker, who saw himself as only a taker, had given to his Dawn. It felt good, and right, and real. It was too late to turn back. He'd declared his love, and there was nowhere to go but forward.

"So be it," he said decisively. "Oh, Lord, where's the hose? This junk is grim!"

Dawn stripped off her clothes and dressed in blue shorts and a blue and white terry-cloth top. Creed loved her! her heart sang. It was glorious! Nothing could beat them now. Nothing. The ghosts of Creed's past didn't stand a chance because they were together, united, in love.

Dawn brushed her hair to a shimmering, honey-colored cascade that tumbled down her back. With a smile on her lips she dashed from the room to go to Creed.

He stood waiting for her, his clothes and shoes soaked with water, and circled her shoulders tightly with his arm as she moved to his side. They shared a warm smile, a tender gaze, then walked without speaking through the woods to their private place by the swimming hole. Creed pulled her down next to him on the plush grass and kissed her deeply.

"I want to make love to you," he said, close to her lips, "but we have to talk."

"Couldn't we talk later?" she asked, undoing the buttons on his damp shirt.

"No!"

"Pooh."

"Dawn, I want you to understand something. I didn't intend to tell you that I loved you until I was free of my past, was a whole man again. I also realized that it might never happen, that I might never find the peace I'm seeking. But now everything has changed, because I *did* tell you how I feel."

"Thank goodness," she said, leaning her head on his shoulder.

"I've got that Ping-Pong ball in my head again, but at least it's slowing down a little, giving me a chance to catch my breath. I've had a glimpse of it, Dawn, the peace, here on the farm. Being with you, working the land, has given me the beginning of a sense of purpose. I'd decided that allowing you to warm my inner chill was wrong, totally unfair to you. I'm probably right, but I can't stop it from happening."

"It isn't wrong, Creed. You give that same warm glow to me."

"Yeah, well, you were doing all right before I got here. I arrived in the form of an empty bucket. I'm still not in that great shape. You've got to realize that a section of me is dead, gone, lost. I want to be complete for you, but it might never come to be. All I have to offer you is what's left, what you see, part of a man. That's it. That, and my love."

"Oh, Creed," she said, tears shimmering in her eyes as she lifted her head to look at him, "I love you so much. We can find your peace together, put the past away."

"Maybe not! That's the point, don't you see? I've got to know that you understand that it might not happen! You'd be waiting, watching, for some signal that everything was suddenly terrific. I need you to accept me just as I am right now, because this might be the best I can do. I may have to live with my past for the rest of my life. Can you do that, Dawn? Share me with ghosts?"

No! her mind said.

Yes! said her heart, and Yes! said her soul.

And Yes! said the very essence of her being, which loved Creed Parker with an intensity that was beyond description in its magnitude.

"Yes, Creed," she whispered.

He drew a deep breath and stared at the sky for a long moment. "I don't deserve you, your love," he said, his voice gritty, "but God help me, I can't let you go. I want so much more for you. I'll try to make you happy, I swear it. Dawn," he said, shifting toward her and cupping her face in his hands, "I'm hoping you won't go with Paul Matts. Stay with me, please? Dawn, I'm asking you to marry me."

"I—"

"For better or worse," he rushed on, "and I'm afraid you're getting the worst. I'm not leaving here, Dawn. I'm going to tend the land, work the farm like a true Parker son. And that's another thing. With me, you get Max. I don't even know how much care he's going to need or... Ah, hell, you'd be out of your mind to marry me!"

"Then color me crazy, Parker!" she said, smiling at him.

"I beg your pardon?" he said, squinting at her. "Does that mean you will? You'll marry me?"

"Yes." She kissed him. "I will." She kissed him again.

Then *he* kissed *her*.

With a moan that rumbled up from his chest, Creed's mouth swept over hers as he lowered her to the plush grass. He drank of her sweetness as his tongue met hers. The shudder that ripped through him was one of desire, need, want. The kiss grew urgent, frenzied. They moved away only long enough to shed their clothing, then reached for each other.

Then Creed slowed the tempo. Mustering every ounce of his control, he kissed and caressed Dawn in a languorous journey over her satiny skin. He thought only of her, placing her pleasure before his own, wanting to give, *give*, to this woman who had given so very much to him.

"Oh, Creed!"

"Soon," he said, drawing the bud of her breast into his mouth.

His muscles trembled from the effort of his restraint, his body shone with glistening perspiration, his heart thundered in his chest. But still he held back.

Dawn tossed her head restlessly as her fingers dug into Creed's corded shoulders. Heat licked throughout her, igniting the flame of passion. She moaned in mingled pleasure and pain, and called Creed's name in a voice husky with desire. She needed him *now* to fill her with his masculinity, consume her, quell the fire that burned within her.

"Creed!"

"Yes!"

He entered her with a smooth, powerful thrust that took her breath away. She arched her back to meet his driving force, matching his rhythm, taking him deeper and deeper within her. She was him. He was her. They were one. And it was ecstasy.

Seconds apart, the crescendo was reached in a maelstrom of sensations that rocketed through them. The earth beneath them seemed to shift, tilt, hurl them into an abyss of splendor from which they did not wish to return. They held fast to each other, lingered there beyond reality, then slowly, reluctantly drifted back.

Creed pushed himself up to rest on trembling arms, then kissed Dawn's lips, cheeks and forehead, before moving away and pulling her close to his side.

"Incredible," she said softly.

"Beyond words," he said, sifting her hair through his fingers.

They lay quietly, bodies cooling, heartbeats returning to normal levels, as the sounds of nature serenaded them.

"Creed," Dawn said finally, "why were you in such a hoopla over Paul Matts?"

"Elaine said it would serve me right when you packed up and went with him. I freaked out, I guess. I couldn't handle the thought of you leaving me."

"But I told Elaine and Orv at dinner last night that I had no intention of accepting that offer. Did Elaine actually tell you I was going?"

"Yes. Well, no, maybe not. I think I was had."

"And I'm glad. It brought you storming through the woods like a crazy man and you told me that you love me. What more could a girl want?"

"A baby."

"What?!"

"Sorry. My mind is jumping all over the place. I was thinking it would really be something if you and I had a baby. Am I rushing you?"

"Just a tad," she said, laughing softly. "We're not married, remember? I have a tendency to be slightly old-fashioned about motherhood. Not prudish, you understand, simply conventional."

"Good point. We'll get married right away. But, Dawn, I'd never want our child to know that his father had been a ... I couldn't tell him."

"Say the word, Creed. Say, 'killer,' and then really listen to it. It indicates a cold-bloodedness, a ruthlessness, a total disregard for human life. The title doesn't fit you. It doesn't! Yes, you killed with that gun, but only to stay alive. You acted on behalf of your country, on assignments given to you by your government. You did nothing wrong, except not listen to your inner voice when it said you'd had enough. That was your only mistake, Creed."

"You don't understand," he said, sitting up and reaching for his clothes. "I felt nothing toward the end when I killed those men. I just walked away as though it had never happened. That makes me a killer, Dawn, so don't try to pretend otherwise. Facts can't be changed."

"But men can change, and you did. You came home."

"With the ghosts."

"Yes," she said, sighing, "with the ghosts."

"Hey," he said, pulling her up to sit beside him, "let's give all this a rest. This is supposed to be a happy occasion. We're in love, we're going to be married, and make beautiful babies together."

"You betcha, Farmer Parker. Oh, Creed, I do love you so much."

"And I love you," he said, kissing her deeply. "Come on," he added, when he finally released her, "let's go find Orv and sneaky Elaine, and tell them the good news. You realize, of course, I'm only marrying you because I can't get the hang of this cooking number."

"Sure, I know that."

"And because," he said, serious again, "you are the most wonderful thing that has ever happened to me. You are my gift from the dawn, and I will love and cherish you for the remainder of my days."

"Oh, Creed," she said, blinking back her tears. "Let's go home."

It almost seemed like a dream.

Dawn stood staring out of her window at the night, unable to sleep. The events of the day replayed over and over in her mind, and a smile came to her lips. She was going to marry Creed Maxwell Parker. He wanted her to stay with him on the farm, marry him, have his baby. It was glorious!

Elaine and Orv had been thrilled. Elaine had, Dawn mused, been slightly smug, as if she were taking credit for the whole thing. And Max. Dear, sweet Max had gotten tears in his eyes when she and Creed had shared their news when they'd visited him. Even Dr. North had looked happy, and said Max could come home the next day, ahead of schedule.

Dawn and Creed had gotten blood tests at the open clinic at the hospital, then had gone for the postponed ice cream soda to discuss when they could get married. Max's health had been an important consid-

eration, they both agreed, and they'd settled on asking the minister who had the small rural church if he
would perform the ceremony in the Parker living
room. The clergyman was on vacation, the secretary
had said, but she would write the Parker wedding on
the calendar.

"Two weeks," Creed had grumbled. "Ministers
aren't supposed to go on vacation. What if somebody
dies, or has a problem, or ... or whatever?"

"Or wants to get married," Dawn had said, laughing.

"Yeah! Exactly. The man has a responsibility to his
congregation!"

"The man has a right to a vacation like everyone
else."

"I waited thirty-five years to get married, and I
want to do it now!" Creed had said fiercely, then or-
dered another ice cream soda to make himself feel
better.

And then the wedding rings. Lovely brushed-gold
matching bands, Creed's twice as wide as Dawn's, and
both nestled in a blue velvet box. Dawn had held them
all the way home, then pouted when Creed said to
cough them up until he could officially put hers on her
finger.

The dinner at Elaine and Orv's had been festive,
then Dawn had come back to the Parker farm with
Creed to help him milk the cows. Then in Creed's bed,
where she had first seen him as the beautiful bum, they
made sweet, slow, sensuous love. With obvious reluc-
tance they got dressed again and Creed walked her
home through the woods, mumbling about the irre-
sponsibility of ministers who went on vacation. After

one last searing kiss and shared declarations of love, they parted.

Now, near midnight, Dawn was unable to sleep. An infinite joy filled her, an indescribable happiness. Everything was wonderful, fantastic, marvelous.

Except for Creed's ghosts.

She sighed, then crawled back into bed. It wasn't fair, she mused, that a man who had given so much to his country should suffer such an aftermath of pain. Creed deserved to be free of his past, to move into his future whole, as he yearned to do.

At the swimming hole, Creed had sounded almost resigned to his fate of living with demons, as though he were giving up the battle against the dark tunnel. No! He couldn't do that! It wasn't just for herself that she wished him free, but for Creed. And she would help him. Somehow. He'd said she warmed the icy misery in his soul when he was with her, but she knew it crept in around him again when he was alone. It had to be conquered once and for all. She couldn't bear the thought of him suffering. She just couldn't.

"Oh, Creed, I love you so much," she said to the night. "So very, very much."

Creed too, was awake. He lay in his bed, missing Dawn. Her aroma was there, the memory of their lovemaking was there, but *she* wasn't there.

What a day, he thought ruefully, running his hand down his face. A crazy bunch of hours, and the bottom line was, he was getting married. Unreal. And fantastic! Lord, how he loved his Dawn, and she loved him, she really did. He also knew that marrying her was probably the most selfish thing he had ever done. That thought caused the knife to twist in his gut again.

How strange life was at times. Years ago he had chosen a path, and his lies had protected his parents from knowing the truth about their son. No one had been hurt. Except himself, of course.

But now? Years later, Dawn was paying the price for his actions. Into their marriage, their private place, their union, he would bring his ghosts. Damn! Why wasn't he stronger than this? Why couldn't he shut the door on his past once and for all, and forget it? He could still feel the cold, heavy metal of that gun in his hand. Dawn deserved better than what he was! And he was going to marry her anyway.

"You're a lowlife, Parker," he said aloud.

With a mumbled expletive, he rolled onto his stomach and finally drifted off to sleep.

"Mighty pretty blue," Max said, standing in front of the house the next afternoon.

Creed chuckled. "Well, don't look at the sides. I have a ways to go yet. I'll do the porch railing and trim in white."

"All spruced up for your bride. That's good, Creed."

"Let's get inside, Dad. It's time you put your feet up."

In the living room, Max settled onto his favorite chair and waved Creed onto the sofa opposite.

"I have questions for you, son," Max said. "I'll only ask them once, and I want straight answers. Fair enough?"

"Yes."

"Do you love Dawn?"

"Yes."

"Do you truly want to stay on the farm?"

"Yes."

"Is a sick old father going to be in your way here?"

"No."

"Have you buried the past, Creed?"

"No, sir, I haven't."

Max nodded, then a silence fell between father and son. Creed waited.

"Fair enough," Max said finally, then got to his feet. "I think I'll go up and rest a bit."

"Dad?"

"Yes?"

Creed pushed himself to his feet and walked to where his father stood. "It's going to be good, Dad," he said quietly. "I love Dawn more than I can tell you, and she loves me. She understands about my ghosts. This home is going to have laughter in it again."

"And children?"

"We hope so."

"Always wanted to be a grandpa. You're taking on a lot of people to love, Creed," Max said, starting up the stairs. "Best do some dusting and cleaning of your soul, so you have room for everyone."

Creed shoved his hands into his pockets and watched until his father disappeared from view.

"Hell of a man," he said under his breath. "Maxwell Parker is something."

"Creed?" Dawn called from the kitchen.

Creed strode into the kitchen, pulled her into his arms and kissed her until her knees trembled.

"Hello," he said, not releasing his hold on her.

"Goodness," she said breathlessly, "that was quite a greeting."

"I missed you. It's been hours since we were at the swimming hole."

"True. How's Max?"

"Doing fine. He likes the blue paint. He went up to his room to rest."

"He volunteered?"

"Yep. I don't think there's going to be any problem with him taking it easy. Seems he always wanted to be a grandpa."

"Really?" she said, laughing in delight. "Sounds good to me. Oh, Creed, I'm so happy, and I'm so glad Max is home where he belongs."

"A lot of new brides wouldn't be so generous about having their father-in-law live with them."

"I love him."

"And I love you. Come sit down at the table. Dawn," he continued, when they were seated, "I called Washington this morning and made arrangements to have my belongings shipped out here. I do own more than one suitcase full of clothes. Truth of the matter is, I have quite a bit of money accumulated. I never had anything to spend it on. I want you to redecorate the house in your own tastes. New furniture, drapes, whatever."

"Your mother put this home together, Creed."

"But it's yours now. Max will want to keep his favorite lumpy chair, but other than that, he won't mind. Will you do it?"

"Well, yes, I guess so. Don't you want an opinion on the furniture I choose?"

"Nope, as long as it's sexy satin and leather. Oh, and maybe a furry rug."

"Sick!"

"I was in this place in Belgium once that . . . Forget it. Lord, I have a big mouth. Want some lemonade?"

"What I want is to hear about Belgium," she said, squinting at him.

"Naw, it's a boring story, really dull. Want to help me paint for a while?"

"Okay. I'm sure your Belgium adventure couldn't have been any racier than mine in India," she said, getting to her feet. "That place was amazing. Absolutely amazing. I was having a marvelous time, until it got raided. Oh, well. Do you want me to paint the porch railing?"

"Raided?" Creed said, a deep frown on his face as he pushed himself up to loom over her. "Why? What kind of place were you in?"

"It wasn't listed in the tourist guide book, I'll tell you that!" she said, laughing merrily as she scooted around him and went out the back door.

"Dawn Gilbert, you come back here!" he yelled, following close behind.

Creed demanded to know all the details about Dawn's escapade in India. She cheerfully refused to utter a word. He waggled a finger at her. She stuck her tongue out at him. He kissed her until she couldn't breathe, and India and Belgium were forgotten. Then they painted the house.

An hour later, Creed came around from the side to where Dawn was standing on the porch painting the railing.

"Nice," he said, nodding. "You do good work."

"I have many talents, Parker," she said, smiling down at him.

"Oh, I know, Gilbert, I know."

"I make cute dolls with freckles, I can cook, the list goes on and on."

"Do tell," he said, chuckling.

"I wouldn't dream of it. There's certain things a lady doesn't discuss while standing on the front porch."

"There's a car coming," he said, raising his hand.

"I don't see... Oh, yes, now I do. You certainly have good ears. Who do you suppose—" Dawn stopped speaking as she looked at Creed, a knot tightening in her stomach as she saw the hard set to his jaw, the rigid, coiled readiness of his muscled body. He'd crossed his arms loosely over his chest, but his hands were clenched into fists. "Creed?" she said, setting down the paintbrush.

"Go in the house, Dawn," he said, his voice low.

"No. I'm not a child, Creed. I'm going to be your wife."

"Go in the house!"

"No!"

"Damn it!"

The black car stopped and a man got out, glancing around the farm as he slammed the door, then started slowly in Creed's direction. He was wearing a tan suit that stretched tightly over a well-muscled physique. Around forty, he had sandy-colored hair peppered with gray, and was perhaps two or three inches shorter than Creed. His features were ruggedly handsome, except for a scar that cut through one eyebrow, and a slight bump on a previously broken nose. He walked with an easy rolling gait, and with each step, Creed grew more tense, his eyes icy chips of winter-blue, as a pulse throbbed in the strong column of his neck. Dawn wrapped her arms around her elbows and chewed nervously on the inside of her cheek, as her gaze flickered back and forth between the two men.

The stranger stopped about three feet from Creed, glanced at Dawn, then the house.

"Nice place," he said. "Doing a little painting, I see. Pretty color."

Creed didn't speak.

The sound of Dawn's heartbeat echoed in her ears.

"You led me a merry chase to Greece, Creed," the man said, a casual tone to his voice.

"You can go to hell, Curry," Creed said, his voice ominously low.

Nine

————

Curry! Dawn's mind screamed. Oh, dear heaven, no!

"Now, now, let's not use such language in front of the lady," Curry said, unbuttoning his jacket and shoving his hands into his pockets. "I assume she's your lady, Creed?"

"Not that it's any of your business, but Dawn is about to become my wife," Creed said tightly. "Are you getting the message yet? I'm finished! Done! There is nothing you can say that will change my mind, not this time."

"I see," Curry said. "Well, perhaps Dawn will excuse us so we can discuss this privately."

"No way," Creed said. "She knows what I've done. I told her, just the way you chose to tell my father."

"So, now you're just one big happy family," Curry said. He smiled, but no warmth reached his dark eyes. Dawn shivered. "Very touching, Creed," Curry continued. "Killer turns farmer. What's next? You sit in a rocker on this pretty porch of yours and write your memoirs?"

"Shut up and get off my land," Creed said, his eyes narrowing. "Now!"

"Hey, is that any way to talk to a man who saved your life a couple of times?"

"And I saved yours! We're even, Curry. All the way across the board. I don't owe you a thing. I walked away from the stinking world you live in, and I'm not going back!"

Yes, that's right, Dawn thought frantically. Creed was home, and he was staying on the farm! Curry had to go away! Go away and leave them alone!

"I'm beginning to think you mean it, ole buddy," Curry said, pulling his hands from his pockets and crossing his arms over his chest. "Thing is, the slate isn't as clean as you think. I never thought you'd cop out leaving a debt, Creed. I never thought you'd do that."

"What in the hell are you talking about?" Creed growled.

"You do remember that last little fiasco we were in, don't you? Sure you do, because that was when you lost it. The kid cried his little heart out and you let him off."

"So? Let the courts handle him."

"I was yelling at you to shoot him because my gun had jammed. Didn't you hear me?"

"Not really, and I'm not listening to you now."

"You should have killed him, Creed," Curry said, shaking his head. "I saw in his eyes what you would have seen if you hadn't been strung out. The kid was crazy, a fanatic. You know how to tell the difference, but you weren't paying attention. You left unfinished business behind. Because of you, Parker, people are dead!''

It happened so quickly, Dawn hardly saw it. Creed's hands shot out and gripped the lapels of Curry's jacket. In the next instant, Creed slammed him roughly against the porch railing, causing Dawn to gasp and jump back in surprise. She stared at the two men, her trembling fingers pressed to her lips in fear.

"I won't fight you, Creed," Curry said. "You're the only man I know who can take me out. Busting my jaw won't change the facts."

"What facts?" Creed said, his voice icy with rage. "Spill it! Fast!"

"Your crybaby escaped two days after you left. He rounded up some sweethearts, and they went on a binge. Bombs, Creed. Bombs in government cars, mail pouches, you name it. Men are dead because you froze, because you didn't shoot that sniffling lunatic when you had the chance! You've got a debt to pay. He's out there, and it's up to you to bring him down!"

"No," Dawn whispered. "Oh, no, please."

Seconds ticked by as emotions played across Creed's tight, angry features. The fury slowly changed to the haunting pain that settled in his eyes. Then a weariness seemed to sweep through him, as he slowly released his hold on Curry and stepped back, taking a shuddering breath.

Curry pushed himself off the railing and straightened his jacket. The silence hung in the air like a crushing weight, and Dawn could hardly breathe. Her mind screamed at Creed to tell Curry to go away, to catch the terrorist himself, and leave them alone!

Creed had given enough! Dear heaven, he'd given them his soul!

"I knew you'd want to do the right thing," Curry said. "I'll meet you at Central Headquarters in three days, then we'll go find your friend. See you soon, Creed. Pleasure meeting you, ma'am," he said, glancing at Dawn.

Dawn hardly heard the sound of Curry's car starting, then being driven away. She stared at Creed, searching his face for some clue as to what he was thinking, feeling. His expression was blank, unreadable, telling her nothing. On trembling legs she moved off the porch to stand in front of him.

"Creed?" she said, her voice a near-whisper.

He looked down at her as though surprised to see her there. "What?" he said.

"Creed, it's a trick, don't you see?" she said, tears filling her eyes. "Curry is trying to lay a guilt trip on you so you'll come back! If you do it, he'll never let you go. There will be another assignment, then another. He can catch that man. Don't let him do this to you, to us! Creed, please! Say something. Talk to me!"

"I'm very tired all of a sudden," he said slowly, as if speaking were a tremendous effort. "Would you mind checking on Max while I put the paint away?"

"Creed!" she said, a sob catching in her throat. "Please!"

"Check on Max, Dawn. Go on."

Tears blurred Dawn's vision as she stumbled up the stairs and into the house. Max was sitting in his chair.

"Oh," she said, coming to a halt and taking a deep breath, "hello, Max. I, um, did you have a good rest?"

"Come sit down, before you fall down. I saw and heard it all, Dawn."

"Oh, Max," she said, walking across the room and sinking onto the sofa, "Curry was so cruel. He... No, this is wrong. You mustn't upset yourself."

"Hush with that nonsense. I'm not the one in trouble here, it's Creed."

"Creed is acting so strangely, Max, like he's numb, in a trance. I don't know what to do! Oh, God, what if he goes? What if he listened to Curry, actually believes it's his responsibility to find that man? I can't tell what he's thinking! Max, we have to stop Creed. We can't let Curry take him from us, because we'll never get him back!"

"There's nothing we can do."

"Don't say that!"

"Dawn, it's up to Creed. Leave him be. He's fighting the toughest battle of his life right now, and he has to do it alone."

"Oh, Max," she said. She slid off the sofa and sat at his feet, resting her head on his knees. "I love him so much. I don't want to lose him."

"I know," he said, stroking her hair. "I know."

A silence fell over the room, then a few minutes later it was broken by the sound of Dawn's crying. She wept as though her heart would break, and Max allowed her to cry out her misery and fear. What she didn't see were the tears shimmering in his blue eyes.

Creed lay on his back on the grass by the swimming hole. He watched the sun skitter through the leaves of the trees, then saw a bird land next to another on a branch. A few moments later they flew away, together.

Every muscle in Creed's body ached, and he ran his hand down his sweat-soaked face with a weary sigh. He had never been so tired, so drained. Breathing was an effort. Curry's words slammed against his brain with an unrelenting force, pounding into his head. He wanted to run, but couldn't move. Had to think, but no thoughts came through the cacophony of Curry's accusations. He needed Dawn, but didn't remember where she was.

With a strangled moan of agony that ripped at his soul, Creed covered his ears with trembling hands.

Tears spent at last, Dawn got to her feet, then hugged Max.

"Thank you," she said. "I'll wash my face and get started on dinner."

"I doubt if Creed will be in, Dawn."

"Maybe not, but I'll have it ready. Besides, you're overdue for some decent food. I'll call Elaine and tell her I'm staying."

Dawn was positive that Elaine was aware that something was wrong, but the older woman didn't press for answers. Dawn left it at that, knowing her tears would begin again if she attempted to discuss what had taken place. She concentrated on the preparing of the meal, glancing out of the window many times for any sign of Creed. He was nowhere to be seen.

The meal was consumed in nearly total silence, except for Max's compliments on the fine cooking. He sipped one last cup of coffee while Dawn cleaned the kitchen.

"The cows are bellowing," she said suddenly. "I forgot about them needing to be milked, and apparently Creed has, too."

"I'd say he has other things on his mind."

"Yes, of course, he does. I'll go tend to the cows right now."

"I wish I could help you, Dawn."

"No. I'm a great cow milker. One of the best. I'll be back in soon, Max," she said, going out the door.

In the barn, Dawn stopped, her breath catching in her throat as she saw Creed. He had a milking stool in his hand and was walking toward the stalls. He spun around as he heard her enter, then stood perfectly still. Their eyes met and held in a long moment, then without speaking he moved toward a cow and settled onto the stool.

Fighting back her tears, Dawn picked up another stool and went to the end of the row where she began to milk. She had seen the fatigue etched on Creed's face, the depth of the pain, deeper than ever before, in his eyes. She longed to run into his arms, beg and plead with him not to go, not to listen to what Curry had said. She wanted to declare her love in a voice loud enough to drown out the echoes of his past. But she had to leave him alone in his battle. She had done all she could do, and the rest was up to him.

I love you, Creed, she whispered over and over in her mind. I love you.

The milking was completed, the cans filled and set in the cooling room. Dawn washed her hands, then stepped aside to give Creed access to the sink. The silence screamed.

"What's that noise?" Creed asked suddenly, causing Dawn to jump in surprise.

"I don't hear anything except the cows," she said.

"I do. It's over by that stack of hay. Stay here."

"Forget it," she said, falling in step beside him. "I don't take orders from you, Parker." Oh, how annoying, she thought. The man had enough problems without her sassy mouth.

"I noticed that, Gilbert," he said, smiling at her. Dawn's heart melted right down to her socks.

Creed hunkered down by the pile of hay and brushed some aside. Dawn peered cautiously over his shoulder, deciding that if there was a snake in there, it would be kinder not to scare it to death. She then silently admitted that she was lying through her teeth. Snakes were not her cup of tea.

"Well, now," Creed said, "look at this."

"A kitten!" Dawn said. "It's so tiny! How do you suppose it got in there? It's eyes aren't even open."

Creed cupped the kitten in his hands and pushed himself up, holding it at eye level.

"It's sick, not breathing well. The mother probably brought it here to die. Animals have an instinct, they know when something is hopeless."

"Then I'm glad I'm not an animal," she said, looking at him steadily. "I won't give up on something or someone I believe in."

"Maybe you should," he said quietly.

"No, Creed, I won't. I love you more every passing minute. That's all I can say to you. I love you, Creed Parker. I know you're in terrible trouble because Curry came here. I also know that I have to leave you alone to deal with it. Just remember..." She brushed a tear off her cheek and continued with a tremor in her voice. "Remember that I love you with every breath in my body. You are my love, my life. Forever."

"Dawn, I . . ."

"Now then!" she said, averting her eyes from his. "Let's see what we can do for this baby. Okay? We'll take it up to the house."

"Dawn, the kitten is dying."

"Well, it's not dead yet! Do you want to help me or not? I'll take care of it myself if you're not interested."

"Lead the way," he said, grinning at her. "I wouldn't dream of crossing you when you're in this mood."

"I should certainly hope not," she said, turning and marching toward the door. She needed him to hold her tightly in his arms, she thought. But at least he was there. And he'd smiled. Oh, Creed!

Dawn was trying so hard to be brave, Creed thought, following her out of the barn. He'd disappeared for hours, hadn't talked to her about Curry, hadn't shared any of his reactions. He was such a louse. The Ping-Pong ball in his mind had gotten a dozen more for company, and he'd finally had to tune out before he lost his sanity. His life, his world, was splintering, crumbling into pieces. Pieces he had so carefully, tentatively begun to build there on the farm with Dawn. What in the hell was he going to do? Bottom line: who owned his soul?

Max was sitting on the back steps and got to his feet when Dawn and Creed approached.

"Sick kitty," Dawn said.

"Yep, looks puny, all right," Max said, peering at the furry bundle in Creed's hands. "Might surprise you, though. Loving goes a long way."

"My sentiments exactly," Dawn said, pulling open the door.

Creed frowned. "You people take a correspondence course in innuendos?" he said.

Max laughed softly. "Well, I'm off to bed. Good luck with the patient."

"Good night, Dad."

"'Night, Max," Dawn said.

"Oh, and, Creed?" Max said, stopping at the kitchen door and turning to look at him.

"Yes?"

"I'd have bet my last ten dollars that you could have knocked Curry out cold. Would I have won?"

"Yes."

"Figured as much. Don't forget about that dusting and cleaning you're supposed to do. 'Night."

"Dusting and cleaning?" Dawn asked, looking up at Creed.

"Of my soul," he said quietly. "Why don't you get a towel for this poor thing, and we'll see what we can do for it."

A half hour later, they sat at the kitchen table staring at the kitten. Creed had brought a gooseneck lamp down from his bedroom, and bent the arm to provide warmth. After Dawn heated some milk, he placed it carefully in the kitten's mouth with an eyedropper.

"What do you think?" Dawn asked.

"It's a fighter, hanging in there. I'll give it milk every half hour."

"All through the night?"

"Well, yeah. It doesn't have enough strength to take much at once. It's the only way. It's going to have every chance to live. I don't want it to die."

Dawn looked at Creed, the kitten, then Creed again. Something was wrong, she told herself. There was a franticness to Creed's voice, a desperate edge, close to panic. But he was the one who had said the kitten was as good as dead. Now he was acting as though the animal was the most important thing going on in his life! Were his emotional burdens so great that he was ignoring them, directing his mental energies toward this helpless creature instead? What was happening to her beloved Creed?

"We could take turns," she said. "Sleep on the sofa in shifts."

"No, I'll do it. I want to."

"Yes, all right," she said, a knot tightening in her stomach. "I'll sleep here on the sofa if you don't mind. I told Elaine I was staying."

"What? Oh, sure, fine," he said absently, his eyes riveted on the sleeping kitten.

Two hours later, Dawn walked wearily into the dark living room and sank onto the sofa. Two hours, and Creed had not spoken to her, nor acknowledged her presence in the room. His attention had centered on the kitten. He had coaxed it to eat, that same frantic edge to his voice when he'd talked to it. It was frightening and confusing, and Dawn was shaken to the core. But in spite of the turmoil in her mind, the events of the exhausting day played their toll and she drifted off to sleep.

"Damn you! No!"

The sound of Creed's voice brought Dawn sitting bolt upright on the sofa. She somehow registered the facts that the clock on the end table said 1:00 A.M., she was on Creed's sofa and he was yelling. She scrambled to her feet and ran into the kitchen.

And then she stopped.

"No," Creed said, placing the kitten gently in the towel and covering it over. "I didn't want you to die. I never wanted anyone to die! I just did what I had to, understand? Do you understand?"

"Creed?" Dawn said, moving to his side. "Creed?"

He turned his head to look up at her.

And he was crying.

He reached for her, circling her waist with his arms and burying his face in her breasts. She cradled his head in her hands as silent tears ran down her face.

"I was doing a job, Dawn," he said, his voice breaking. "I did the best I could. The men I killed wanted to destroy everything this country stands for. God help me, but if I had it to do over, I would."

"Oh, my Creed," she sobbed.

"I will tell—" he drew a racking breath "—I will tell our children that I fought for my country with bravery and honor. And then, when it was time, I came home. My war is over."

He lifted his head to look at her, tears streaming down his face, and shimmering in his eyes. Eyes that were warm, loving, tender, gentle. The winter chill was gone. Creed was free.

"I love you," he whispered.

"Oh, and I love you. Welcome home, Creed Maxwell. Welcome home, my love."

He stood and pulled her to him, holding her tightly. He simply held her as their warmth and strength weaved back and forth one unto the other. It was a moment of sharing like none before, as time lost meaning. The silence was gentle, comforting. They were at peace. The emptiness, the dark tunnel within Creed, had filled with love. They were one.

"Come with me, Dawn," he said finally, "to the swimming hole. We'll take the flashlight and bury the kitten in our private place."

"Yes."

"And then we'll make love under the stars. Oh, Dawn, you've given me so many gifts. Even the gift of learning how to cry the kind of tears you told me about. The kind that cleanse a man's soul. I can love you now, as you deserve to be loved, and I do."

Dawn couldn't speak past the lump in her throat, so she shared a smile with Creed, then he picked up the towel containing the kitten, and they left the house.

Their lovemaking was exquisite. There were only the two of them in a place far removed from reality. Again and again they reached for each other to join as one in a celebration of ecstasy. They slept at last, close, relishing the heat and aroma of each other. The first light of dawn woke them and they greeted the new day filled with the hope and promise of their tomorrows. After dressing, they walked through the woods toward home.

"Creed?" Dawn said.

"Hmm?"

"Since everything is perfect now, I'm feeling guilty about one teeny-tiny, itzy-bitzy thing that I didn't quite tell the truth about."

"Oh?" he said, raising his eyebrows.

"Nothing major, you understand, but maybe it would be better if I were honest about it. Not that it matters, but—"

"Dawn! Spit it out!"

She took off running.

"I've never been to India!" she yelled. "See ya!"

Creed whooped with laughter and started after her, anticipating the moment when he would catch up with his Dawn; his love, his life, his gift.

Silhouette Desire
COMING NEXT MONTH

SECOND WIFE—Stephanie James
Was even friendship too much to expect from Heather after what Flynn had done? He'd loved, then left her, but he soon learned that she was too irresistible for him to stay away.

BRANDED—Gina Caimi
Reporter Ross Baxter assumed it would be easy to trap Sharon Farrell into admitting her husband's death had been no accident. But Ross found himself caught in quite a different trap: love.

NOT AT EIGHT, DARLING—Sherryl Woods
If network VP Michael Compton rescheduled Barrie MacDonald's sitcom out of prime time, the results could be disastrous. Would the magnetic attraction they felt for each other last beyond the season?

LOVE MEDICINE—Suzanne Carey
Diana had been drawn to Rafe years before, but her father had come between them. When the two of them reunited, the feelings were still there, and now they could overcome the obstacles in their path.

BITTERSWEET HARVEST—Leslie Davis Guccione
Six Irish brothers against one lone woman hardly seemed fair, but Andrew Branigan was willing to do anything to keep Holly from selling her land to developers—and to convince her of his love.

CALIFORNIA COPPER—Joan Hohl
The second book in Joan Hohl's Trilogy for Desire. Sculptor Zachery Sharp, the identical twin of the hero of Texas Gold (Desire #294) meets singer Aubrey Mason, the woman who makes him whole.

AVAILABLE NOW:

IN EVERY STRANGER'S FACE
Ann Major

STAR LIGHT, STAR BRIGHT
Naomi Horton

DAWN'S GIFT
Robin Elliott

MISTY SPLENDOR
Laurie Paige

NO PLAN FOR LOVE
Ariel Berk

RAWHIDE AND LACE
Diana Palmer

If you're ready for a more sensual, more
provocative reading experience...

We'll send you
4 Silhouette Desire novels
FREE
and without obligation

Then, we'll send you six more Silhouette Desire® novels to pre-
view every month for 15 days with absolutely no obligation!

When you decide to keep them, you pay just $1.95 each
($2.25 each in Canada) *with never any additional charges!*

And that's not all. You get FREE home delivery of all books as
soon as they are published and a FREE subscription to the Silhouette Books Newsletter as long as you remain a member. Each
issue is filled with news on upcoming titles, interviews with
your favorite authors, even their favorite recipes.

Silhouette Desire novels are not for everyone. They are written especially for the woman who wants a more satisfying, more
deeply involving reading experience. Silhouette Desire novels
take you *beyond* the others.

If you're ready for that kind of experience, fill out and return
the coupon today!

Silhouette ❤ Desire®

Silhouette Books, 120 Brighton Rd., P.O. Box 5084, Clifton, NJ 07015-5084

Silhouette Desire

**Available
October 1986**

California Copper

The second in an exciting new
Desire Trilogy by Joan Hohl.

If you fell in love with Thackery—the
laconic charmer of *Texas Gold*—you're
sure to feel the same about his twin
brother, Zackery.

In *California Copper*, Zackery meets the
beautiful Aubrey Mason on the windswept
Pacific coast. Tormented by memories,
Aubrey has only to trust . . . to embrace
Zack's flame . . . and he can ignite the fire in
her heart.

The trilogy continues when you
meet Kit Aimsley, the twins' half
sister, in *Nevada Silver*. Look for
Nevada Silver—coming soon from
Silhouette Books.

DT-B-1

Silhouette Intimate Moments

Love stories that entice; longer, more sensuous romances filled with adventure, suspense, glamour and melodrama.

She had the pride of Nantucket in her spirit and the passion for one man in her blood.

Until I Return
Laura Simon

Author Laura Simon weaves an emotional love story into the drama of life during the great whaling era of the 1800s. Danger, adventure, defeat and triumph—UNTIL I RETURN has it all!

Available at your favorite retail outlet in OCTOBER, or reserve your copy for September shipping by sending your name, address, zip or postal code along with a check or money order for $7.70 (includes 75¢ for postage and handling) payable to Worldwide Library to:

In the U.S.	In Canada
Worldwide Library	Worldwide Library
901 Fuhrmann Blvd.	Box 2800, 5170 Yonge St.
Box 1325	Postal Station A
Buffalo, NY	Willowdale, Ontario
14269-1325	M2N 6J3

Please specify book title with your order.

 **WORLDWIDE LIBRARY**

UIR-H-1